Billy Tartle in Say Cheese!

By Michael Townsend

Alfred A. Knopf
new york

WHAT'S GOOEY, JUICY, STICKY, AND FUN?
WHY, GOOEY, JUICY, STICKY FUN POPS, of course
THEY'RE Fun-tastic

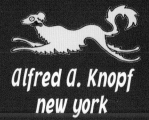

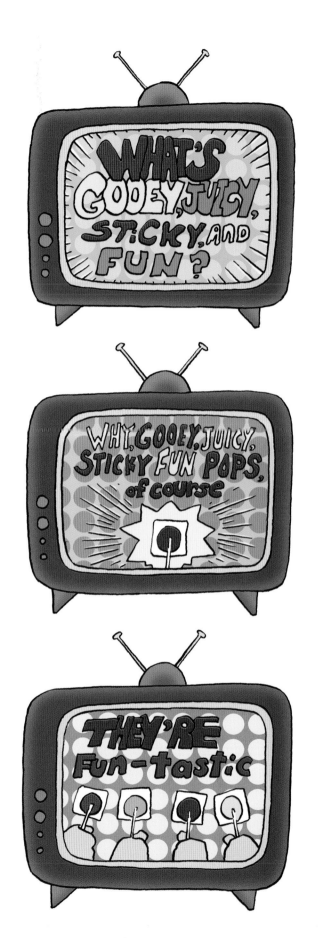

THIS IS A BORZOI BOOK PUBLISHED BY ALFRED A. KNOPF

Text and illustrations copyright © 2007 by Michael Townsend

Published in the United States by Alfred A. Knopf, an imprint of Random House Children's Books, a division of Random House, Inc., New York.

KNOPF, BORZOI BOOKS, and the colophon are registered trademarks of Random House, Inc.

www.randomhouse.com/kids

Educators and librarians, for a variety of teaching tools, visit us at www.randomhouse.com/teachers

Library of Congress Cataloging-in-Publication Data
Townsend, Michael (Michael Jay).
Billy Tartle in Say cheese! / written and illustrated by Michael Townsend.
p. cm.
SUMMARY: Billy is determined to find a way to make his school picture much more memorable.
ISBN 978-0-375-83932-0 (trade) — ISBN 978-0-375-93932-7 (lib. bdg.)
[1. Photographs—Fiction. 2. Schools—Fiction.] I. Title.
PZ7.T6639Bil 2007
[E]—dc22
2006024354

The illustrations in this book were created using black pen and ink and digital coloring.

MANUFACTURED IN CHINA
July 2007
10 9 8 7 6 5 4 3 2 1
First Edition

1 DAY BEFORE PICTURE DAY

SQUEAK-A
SQUEAK-A
SQUEAK-A
WHAT WAS THAT, PROFESSOR CHEW TOY?
SQUEAK-A
SQUEAK-A
YOU'RE SOOO RIGHT! IF I DON'T GET GOING I'll MISS SUPERMONKEY
GOODBYE, PUDDLES!
SLURP

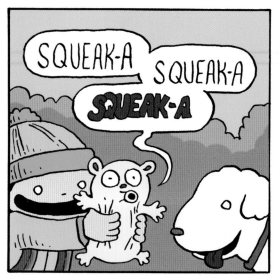

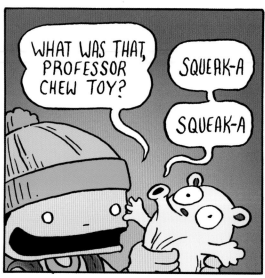

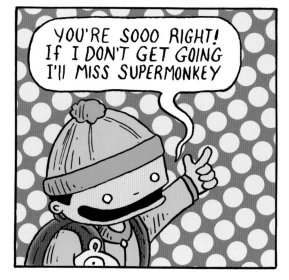

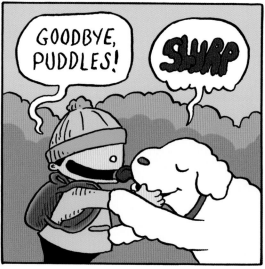

GOODBYE, PROFESSOR CHEW TOY!

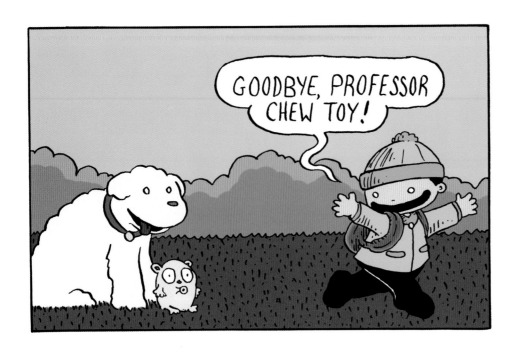

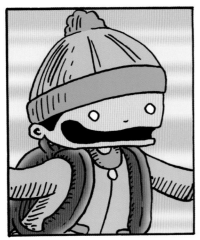

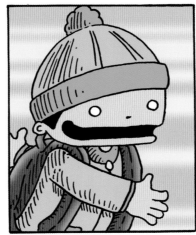

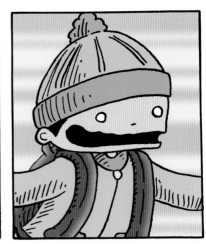

SUPERMONKEY

MOM, I'M HOME!
SUPERMONKEY
SUPERMONKEY
SUPERMONKEY
SUPER SUPER
SUPERMONKEY

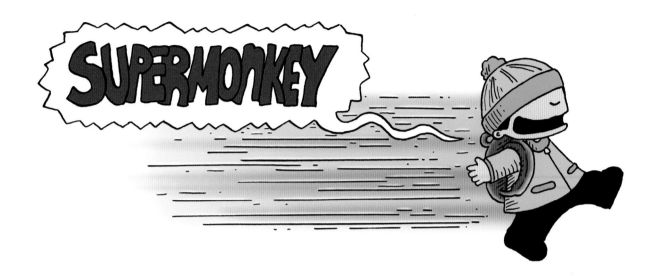

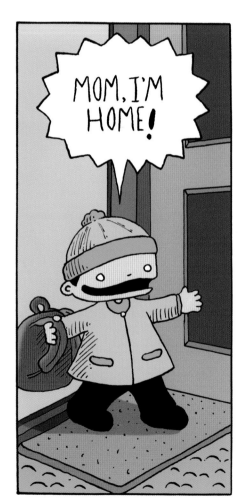

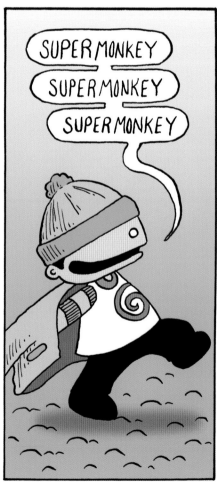

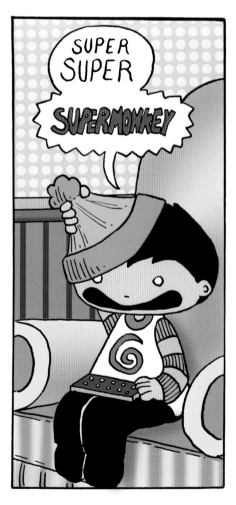

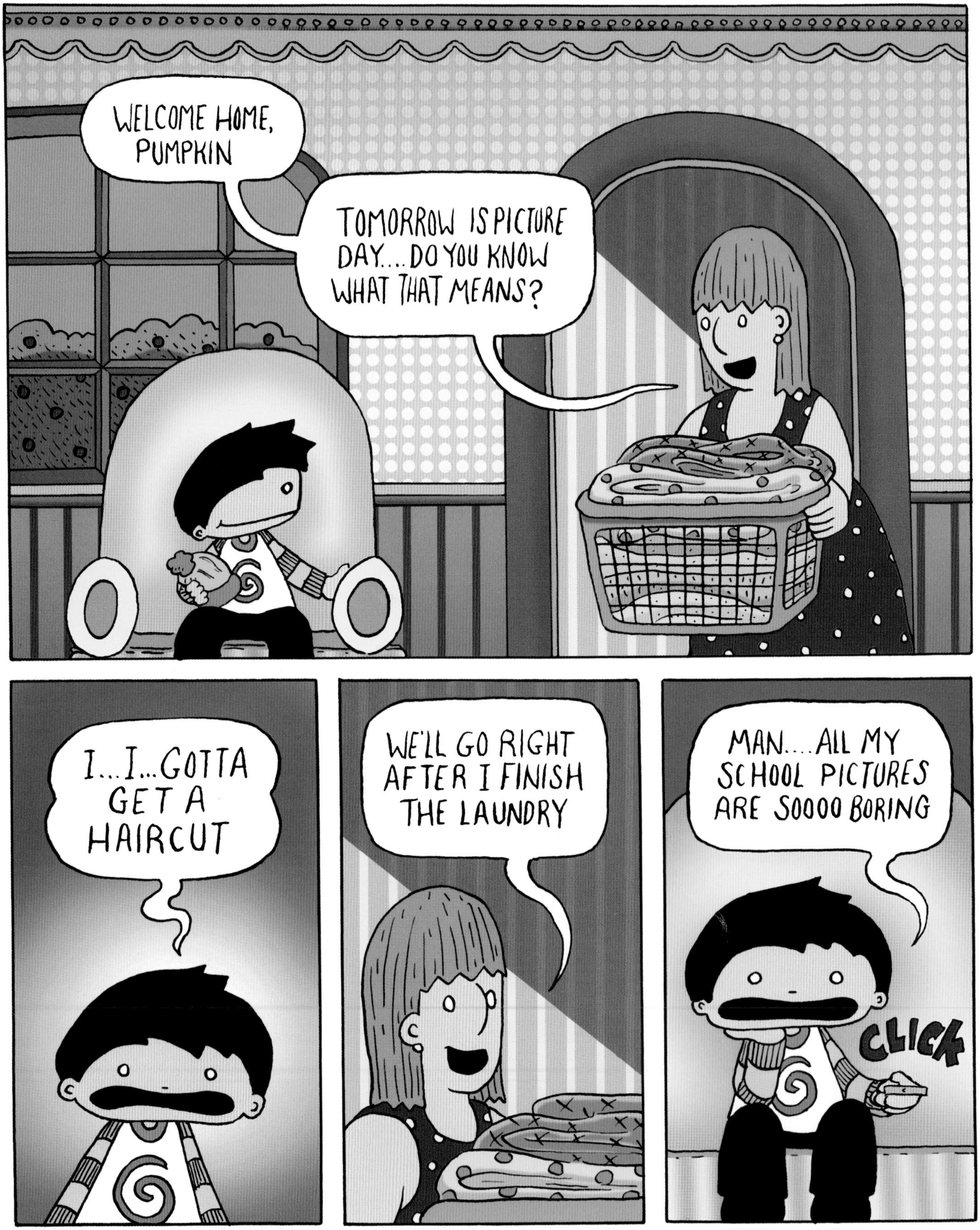
WELCOME HOME, PUMPKIN
TOMORROW IS PICTURE DAY.... DO YOU KNOW WHAT THAT MEANS?
I...I...GOTTA GET A HAIRCUT
WE'LL GO RIGHT AFTER I FINISH THE LAUNDRY
MAN.... ALL MY SCHOOL PICTURES ARE SOOOO BORING
CLICK

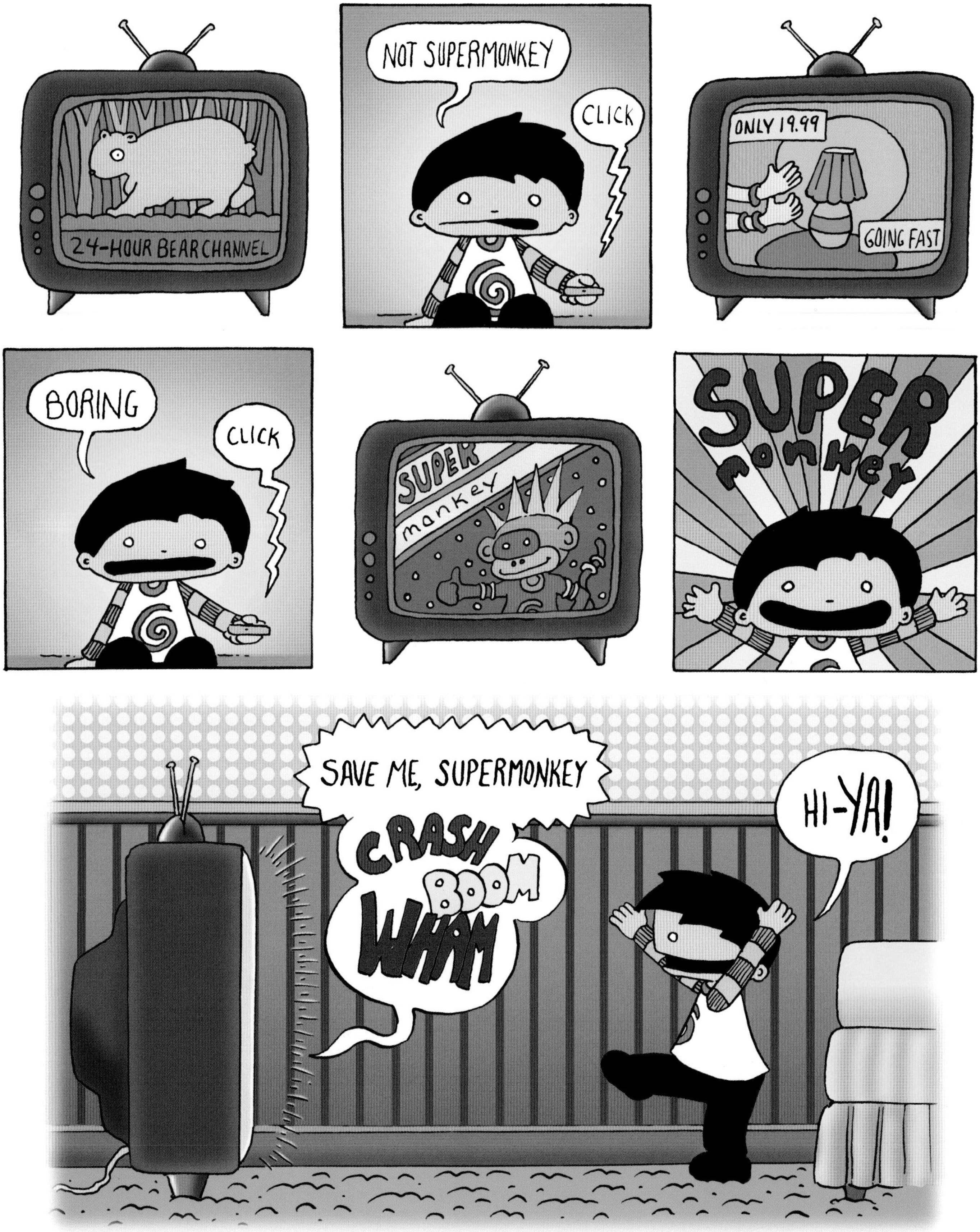
24-HOUR BEAR CHANNEL
NOT SUPERMONKEY
CLICK
ONLY 19.99
GOING FAST
BORING
CLICK
SUPER monkey
SUPER monkey
SAVE ME, SUPERMONKEY
CRASH BOOM WHAM
HI-YA!

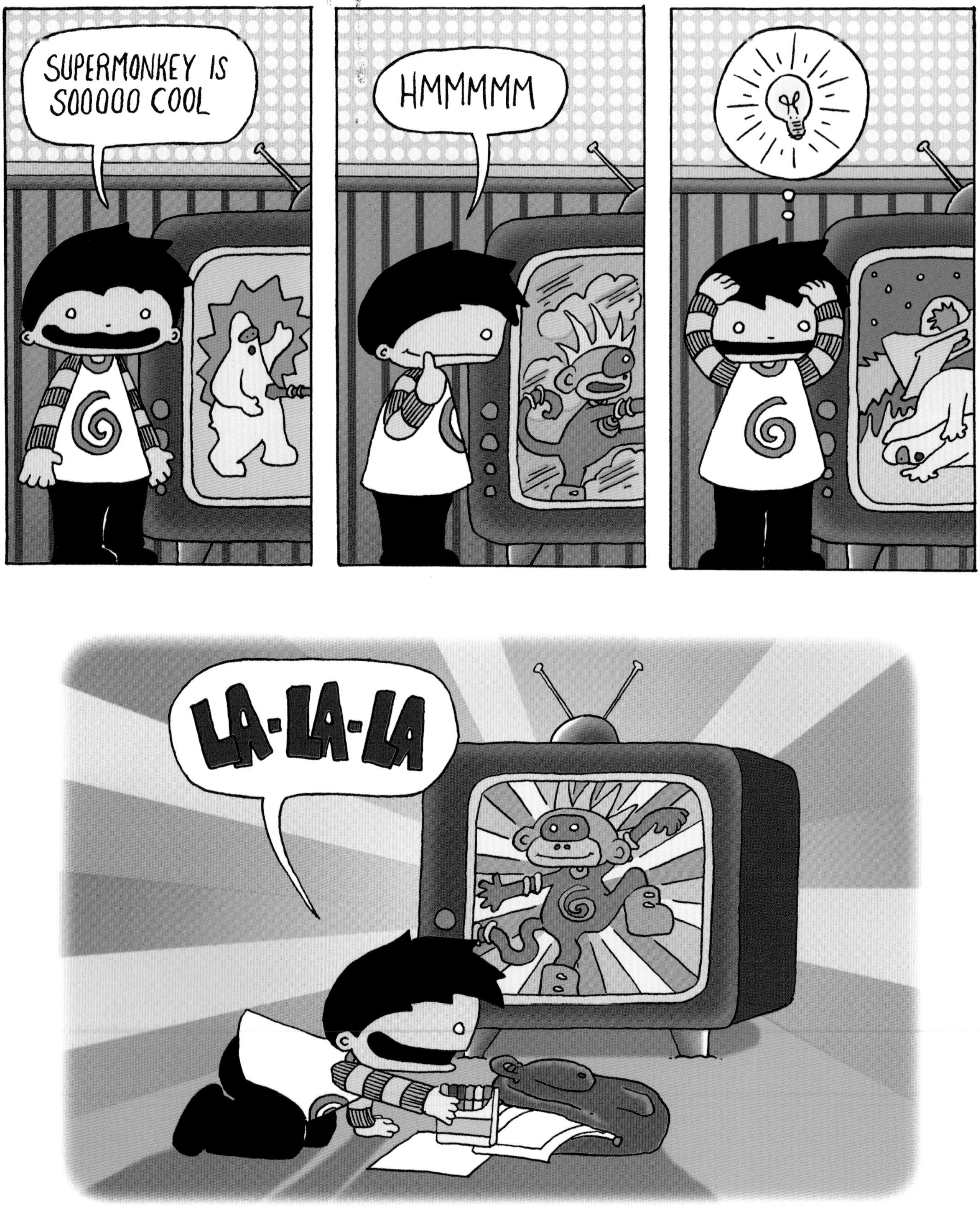
SUPERMONKEY IS SOOOOO COOL
HMMMMM
LA-LA-LA

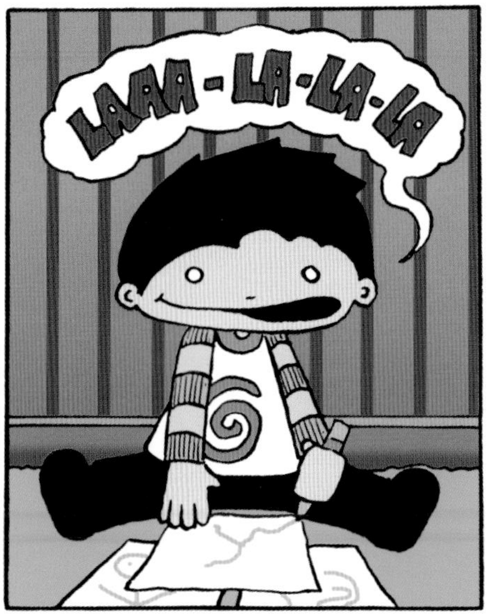
LAAA-LA-LA-LA

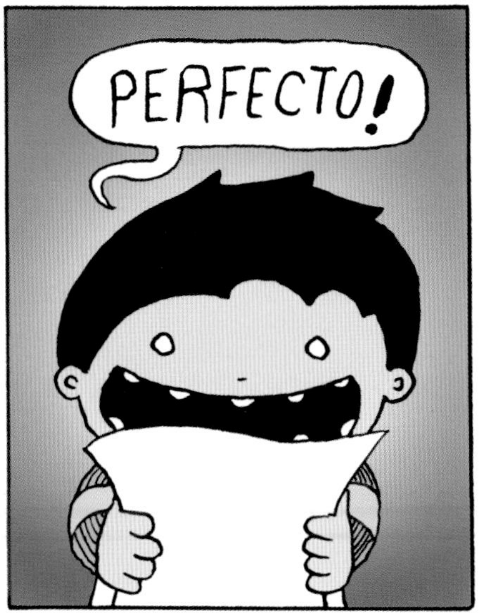
PERFECTO!

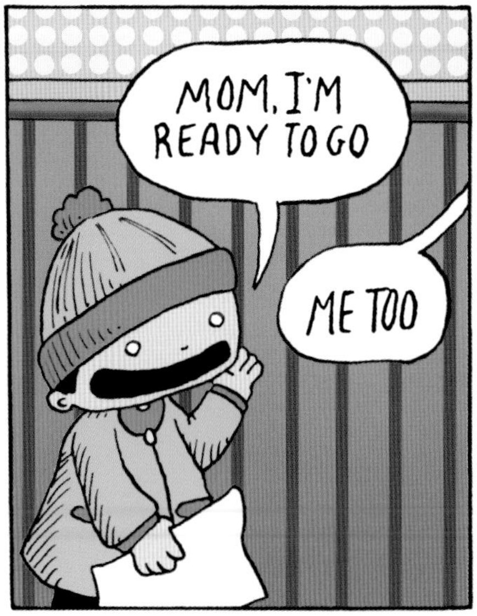
MOM, I'M READY TO GO
ME TOO

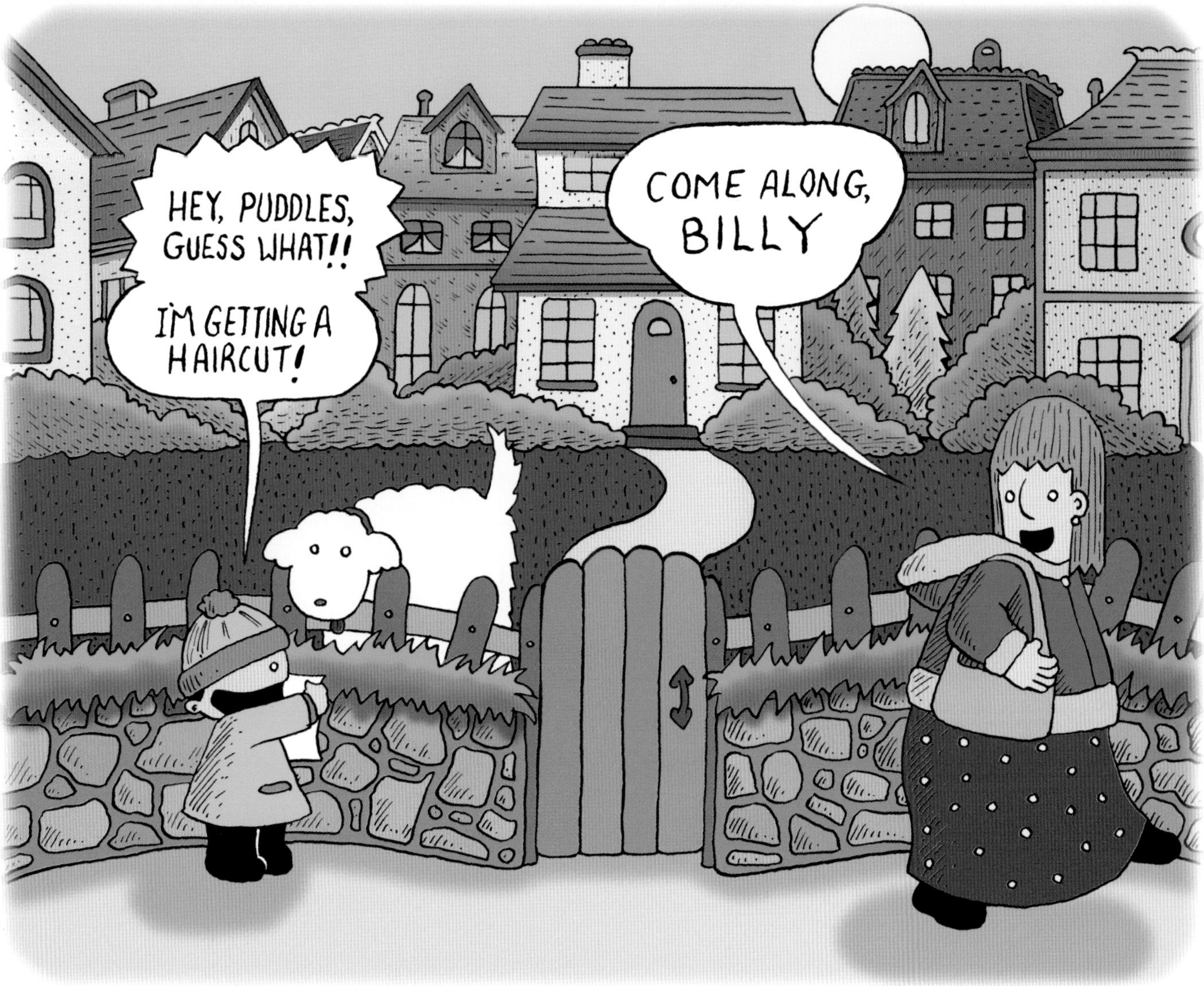
HEY, PUDDLES, GUESS WHAT!!
I'M GETTING A HAIRCUT!
COME ALONG, BILLY

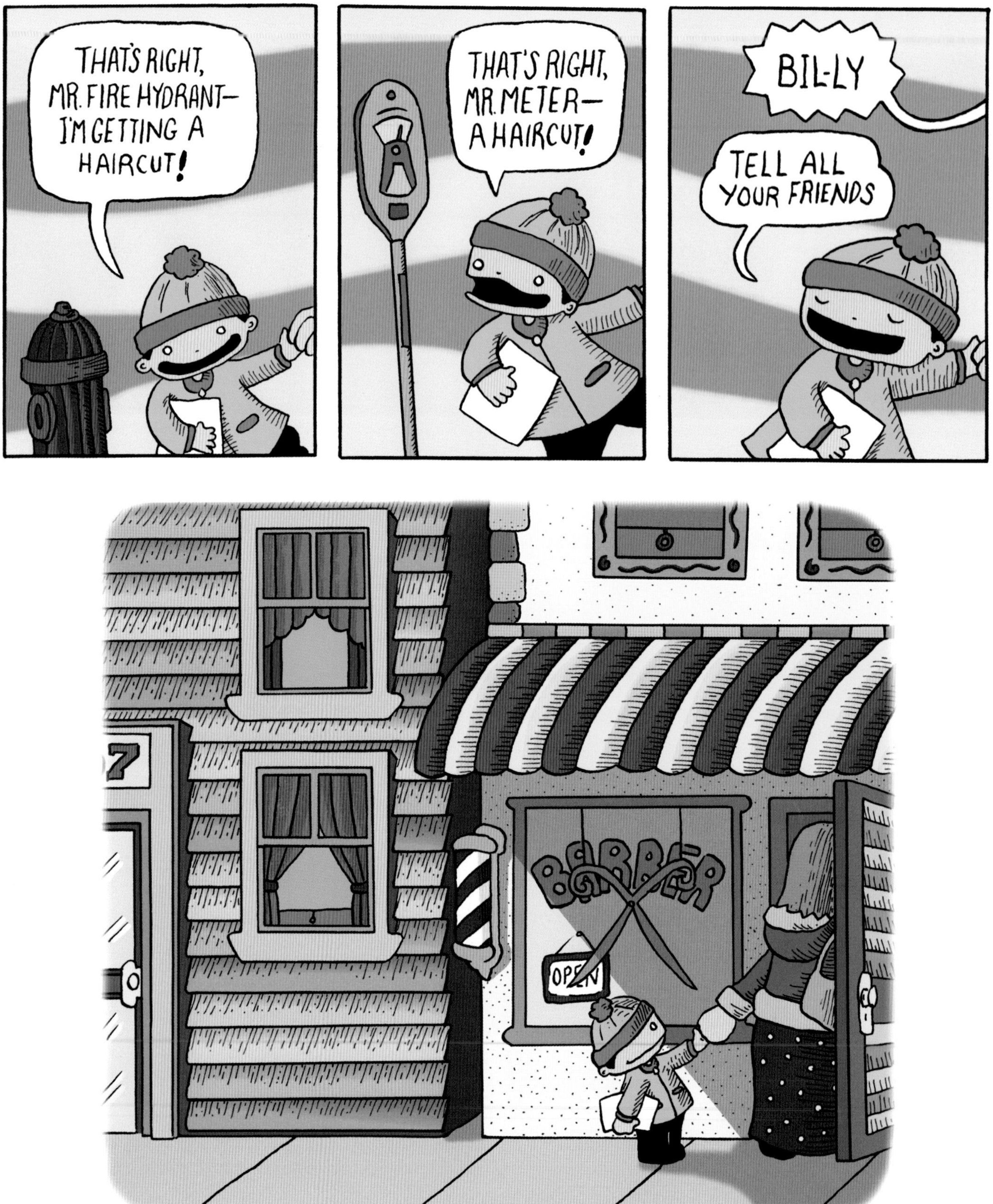
THAT'S RIGHT, MR. FIRE HYDRANT— I'M GETTING A HAIRCUT!
THAT'S RIGHT, MR. METER— A HAIRCUT!
BIL-LY
TELL ALL YOUR FRIENDS
BARBER
OPEN

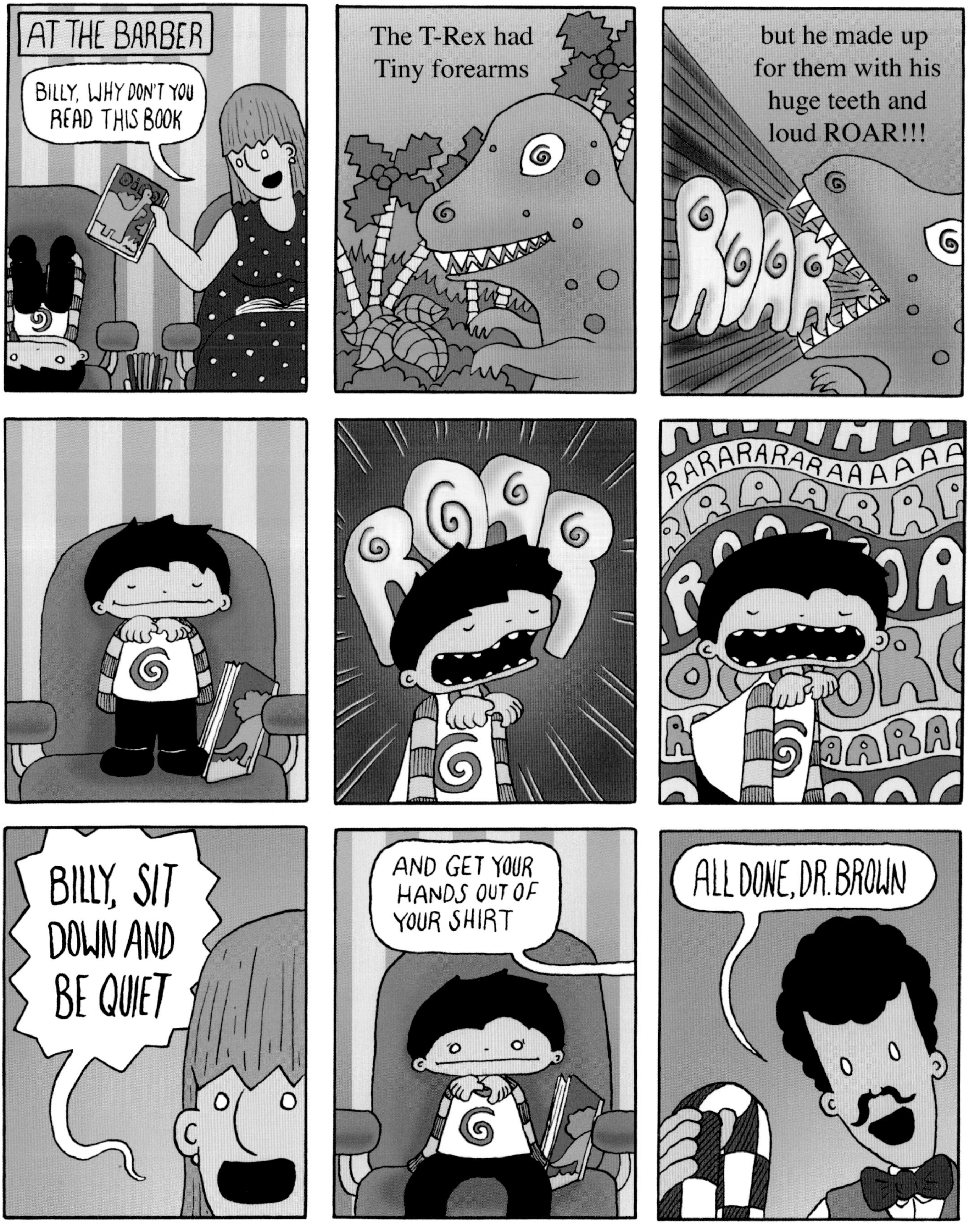
AT THE BARBER
BILLY, WHY DON'T YOU READ THIS BOOK
The T-Rex had Tiny forearms
but he made up for them with his huge teeth and loud ROAR!!!
ROAR
ROAR
RARARARARARAAAAAAA
BILLY, SIT DOWN AND BE QUIET
AND GET YOUR HANDS OUT OF YOUR SHIRT
ALL DONE, DR. BROWN

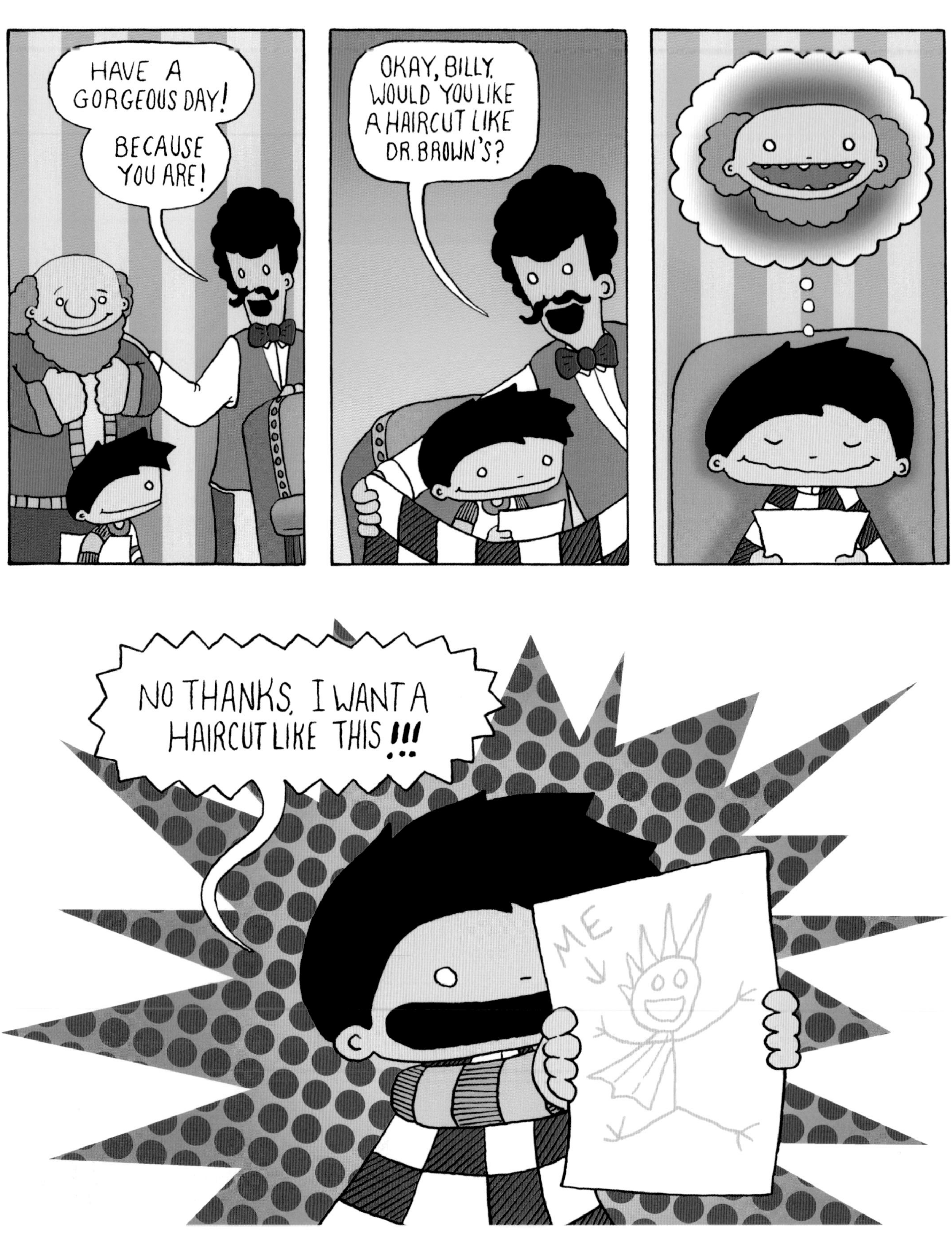
HAVE A GORGEOUS DAY!
BECAUSE YOU ARE!
OKAY, BILLY. WOULD YOU LIKE A HAIRCUT LIKE DR. BROWN'S?
NO THANKS, I WANT A HAIRCUT LIKE THIS!!!
ME

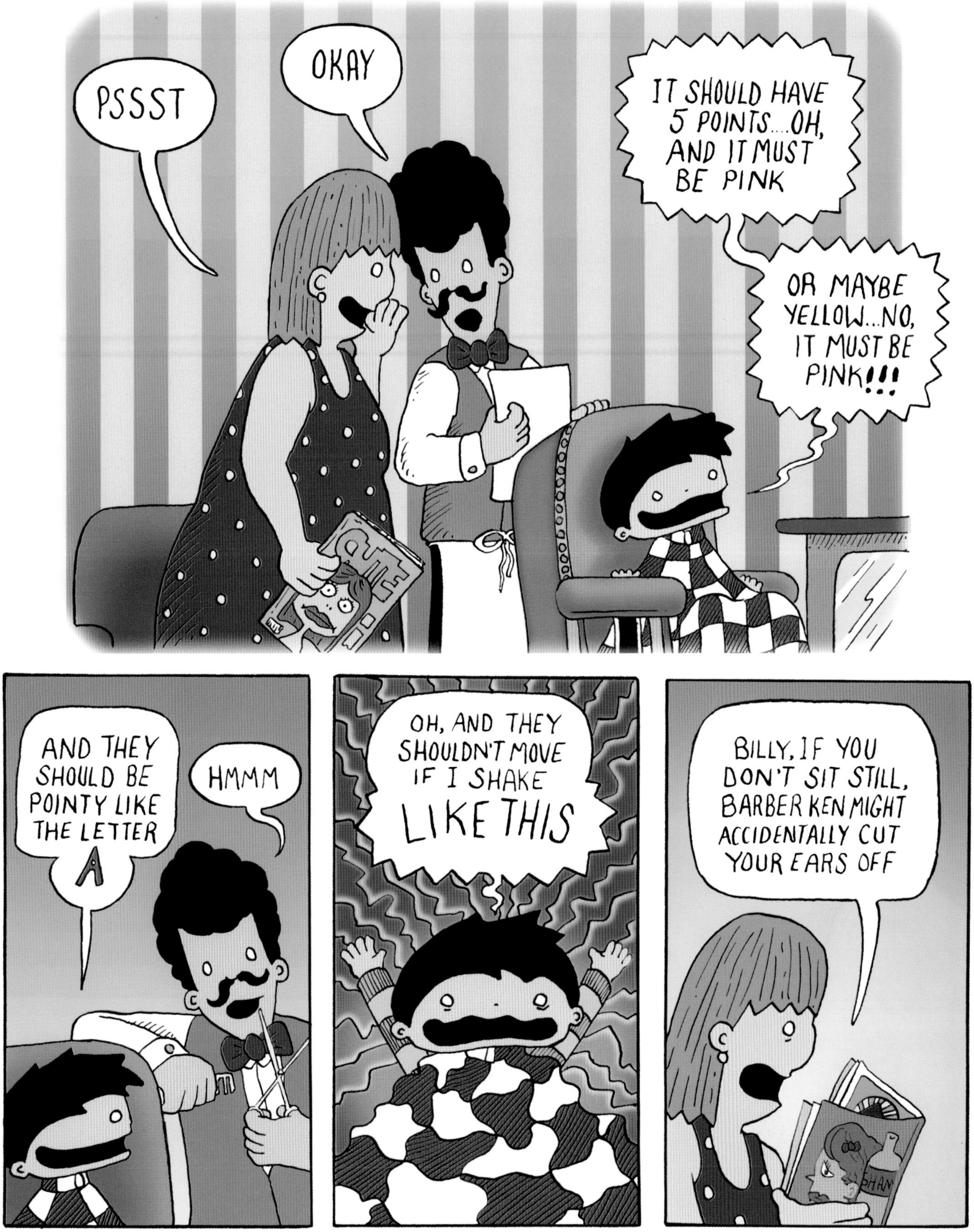
PSSST
OKAY
IT SHOULD HAVE 5 POINTS....OH, AND IT MUST BE PINK
OR MAYBE YELLOW...NO, IT MUST BE PINK!!!
AND THEY SHOULD BE POINTY LIKE THE LETTER A
HMMM
OH, AND THEY SHOULDN'T MOVE IF I SHAKE LIKE THIS
BILLY, IF YOU DON'T SIT STILL, BARBER KEN MIGHT ACCIDENTALLY CUT YOUR EARS OFF

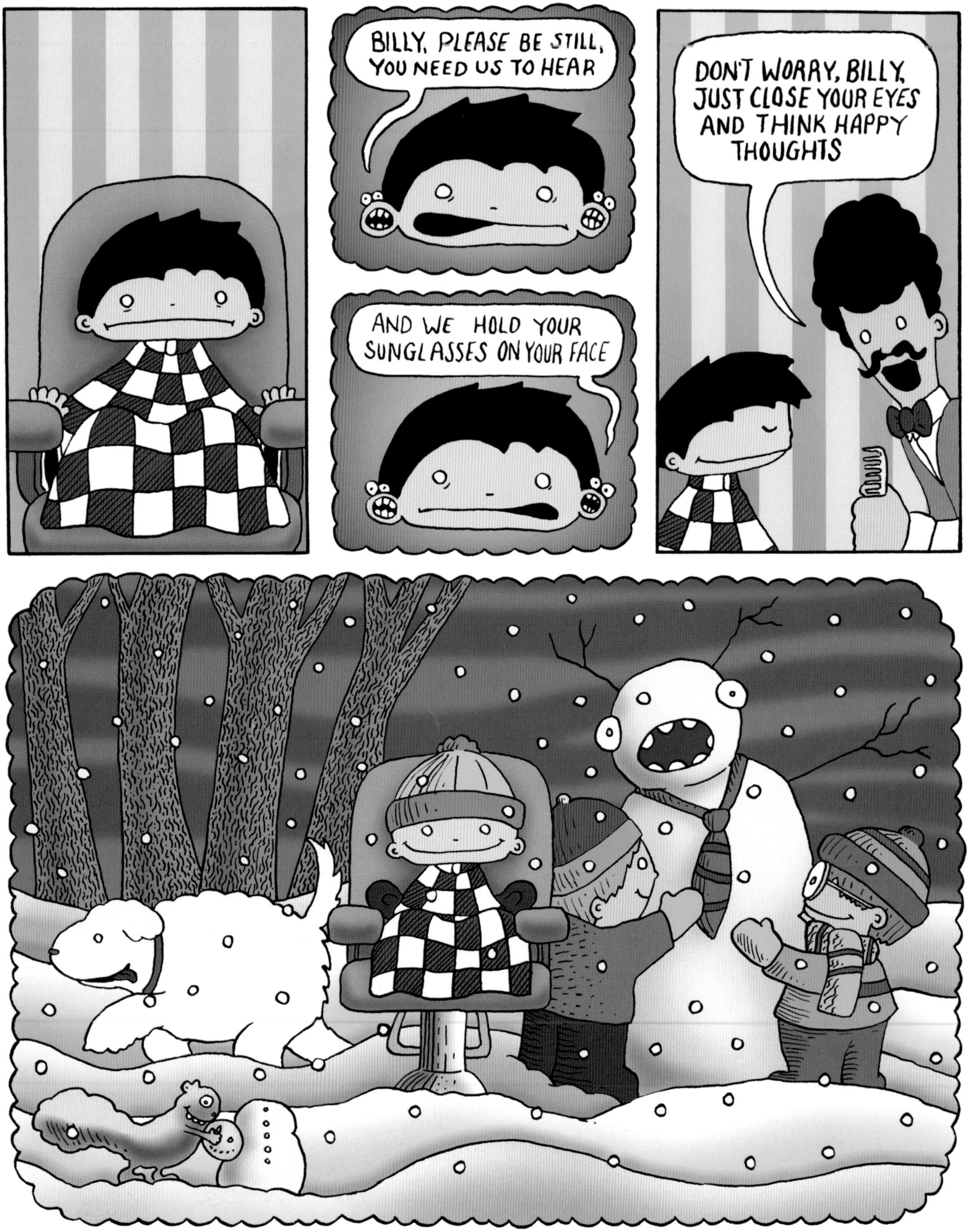

BILLY, PLEASE BE STILL, YOU NEED US TO HEAR
AND WE HOLD YOUR SUNGLASSES ON YOUR FACE
DON'T WORRY, BILLY, JUST CLOSE YOUR EYES AND THINK HAPPY THOUGHTS

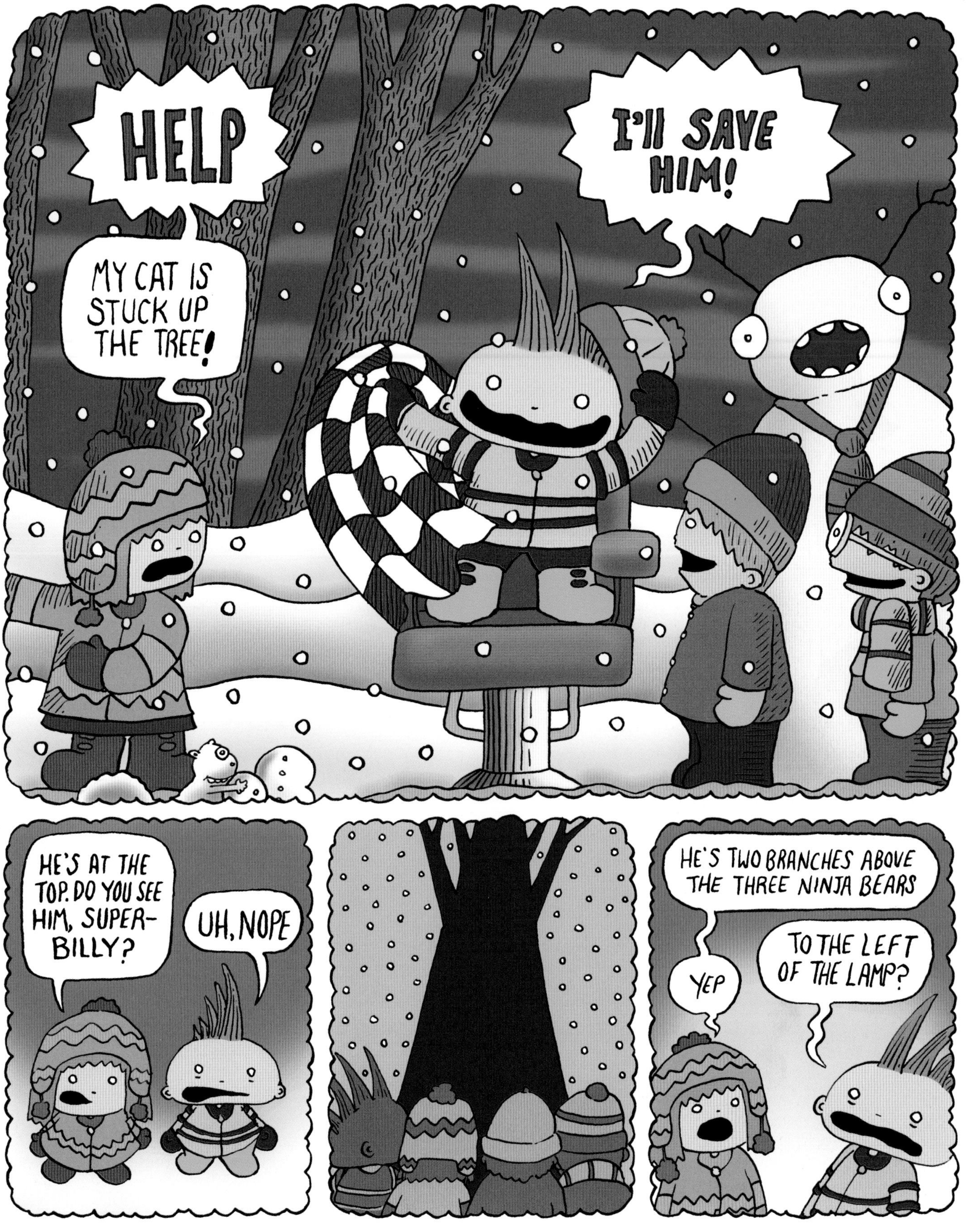
HELP
MY CAT IS STUCK UP THE TREE!
I'LL SAVE HIM!
HE'S AT THE TOP. DO YOU SEE HIM, SUPER-BILLY?
UH, NOPE
HE'S TWO BRANCHES ABOVE THE THREE NINJA BEARS
YEP
TO THE LEFT OF THE LAMP?

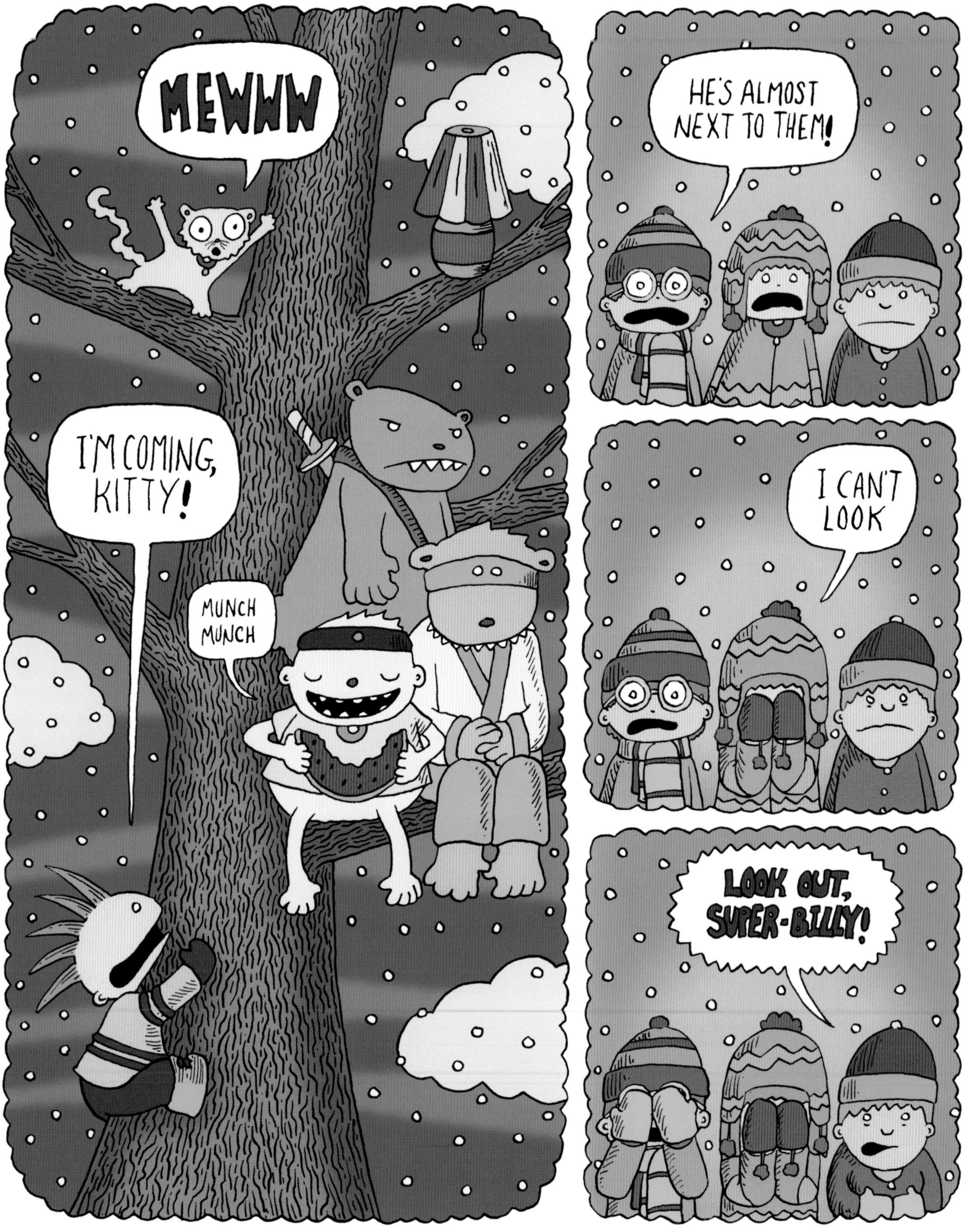
MEWWW
I'M COMING, KITTY!
MUNCH MUNCH
HE'S ALMOST NEXT TO THEM!
I CAN'T LOOK
LOOK OUT, SUPER-BILLY!

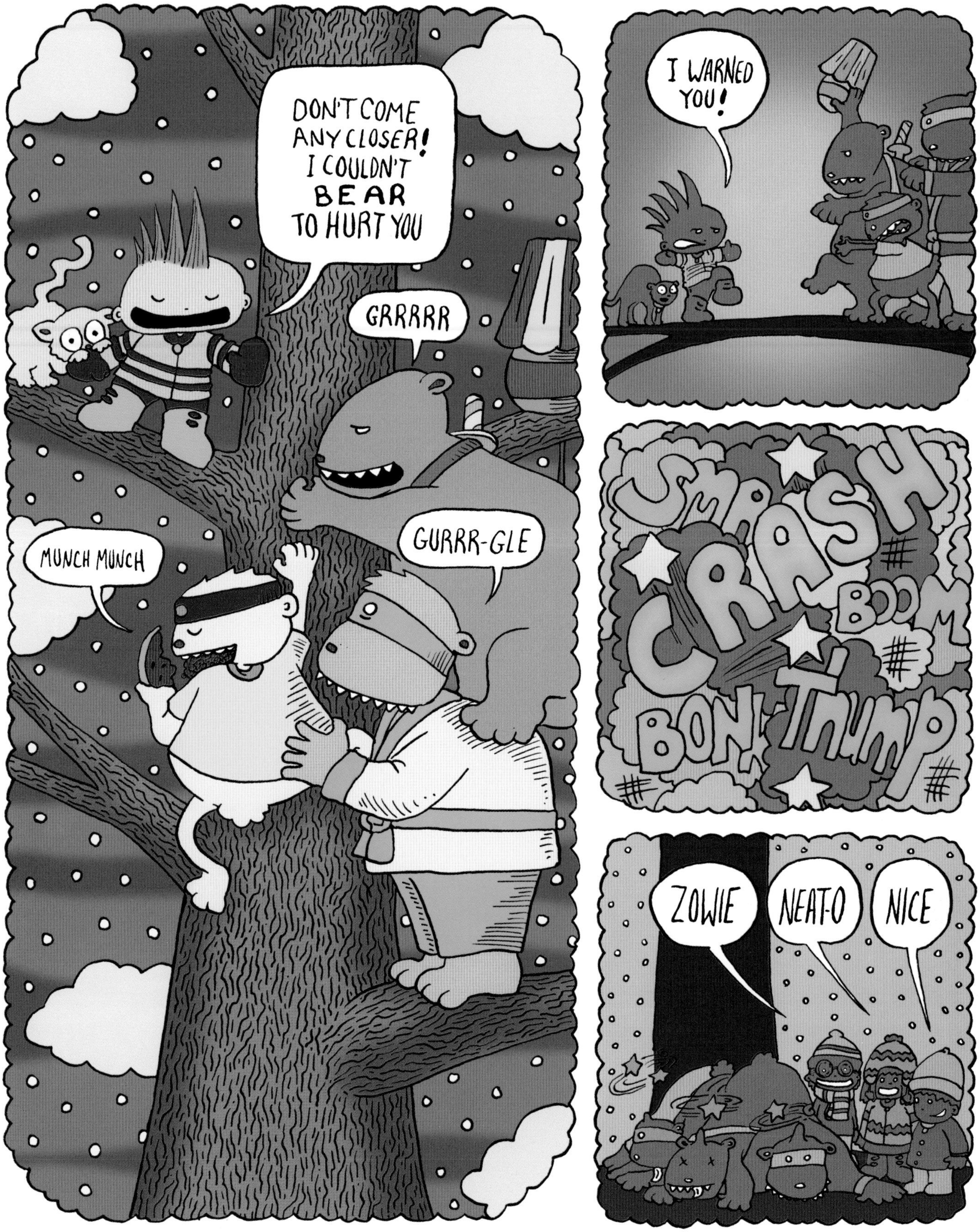
DON'T COME ANY CLOSER! I COULDN'T BEAR TO HURT YOU
GRRRRR
MUNCH MUNCH
GURRR-GLE
I WARNED YOU!
SMASH
CRASH
BOOM
THUMP
ZOWIE
NEAT-O
NICE

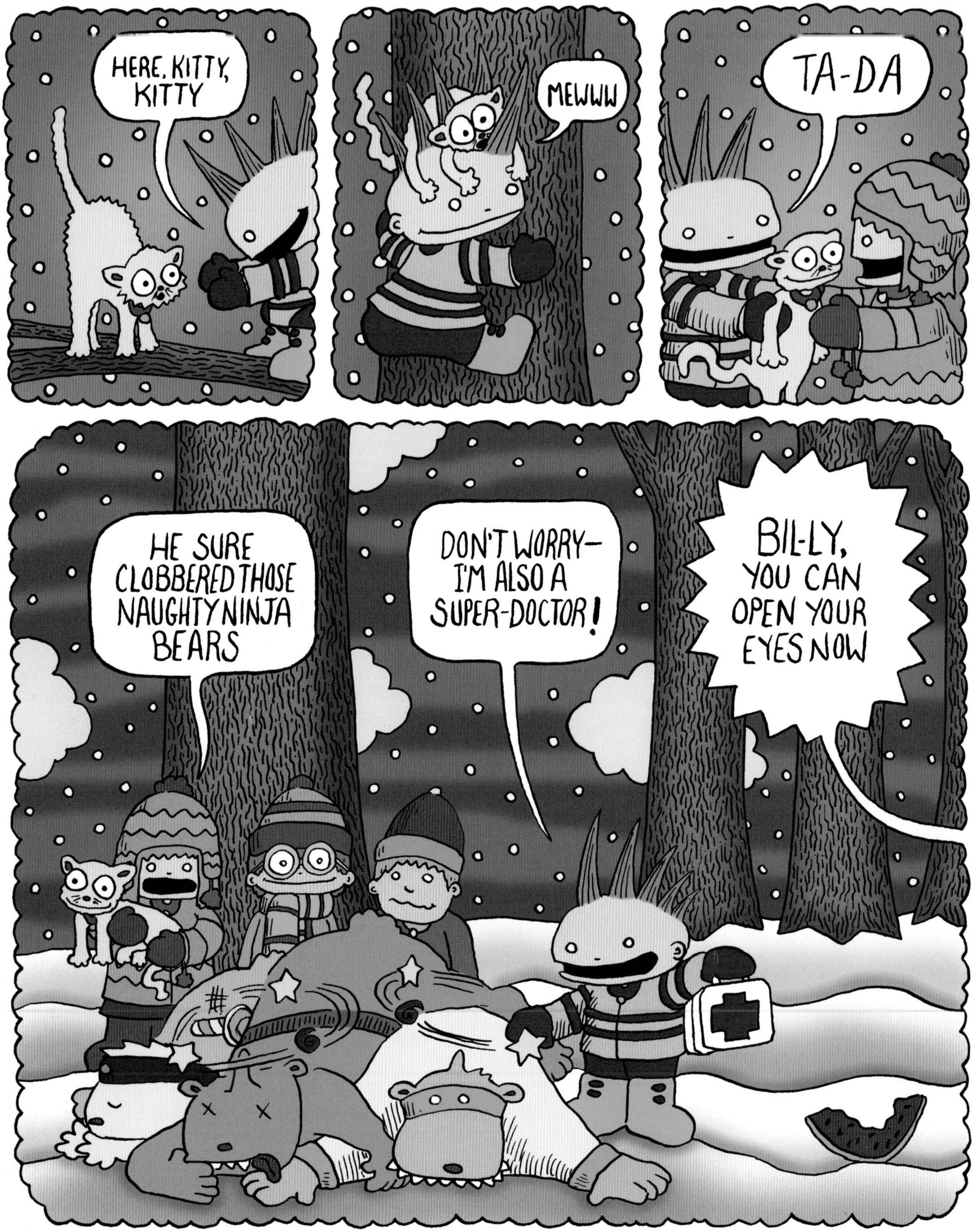
HERE, KITTY, KITTY
MEWWW
TA-DA
HE SURE CLOBBERED THOSE NAUGHTY NINJA BEARS
DON'T WORRY— I'M ALSO A SUPER-DOCTOR!
BIL-LY, YOU CAN OPEN YOUR EYES NOW

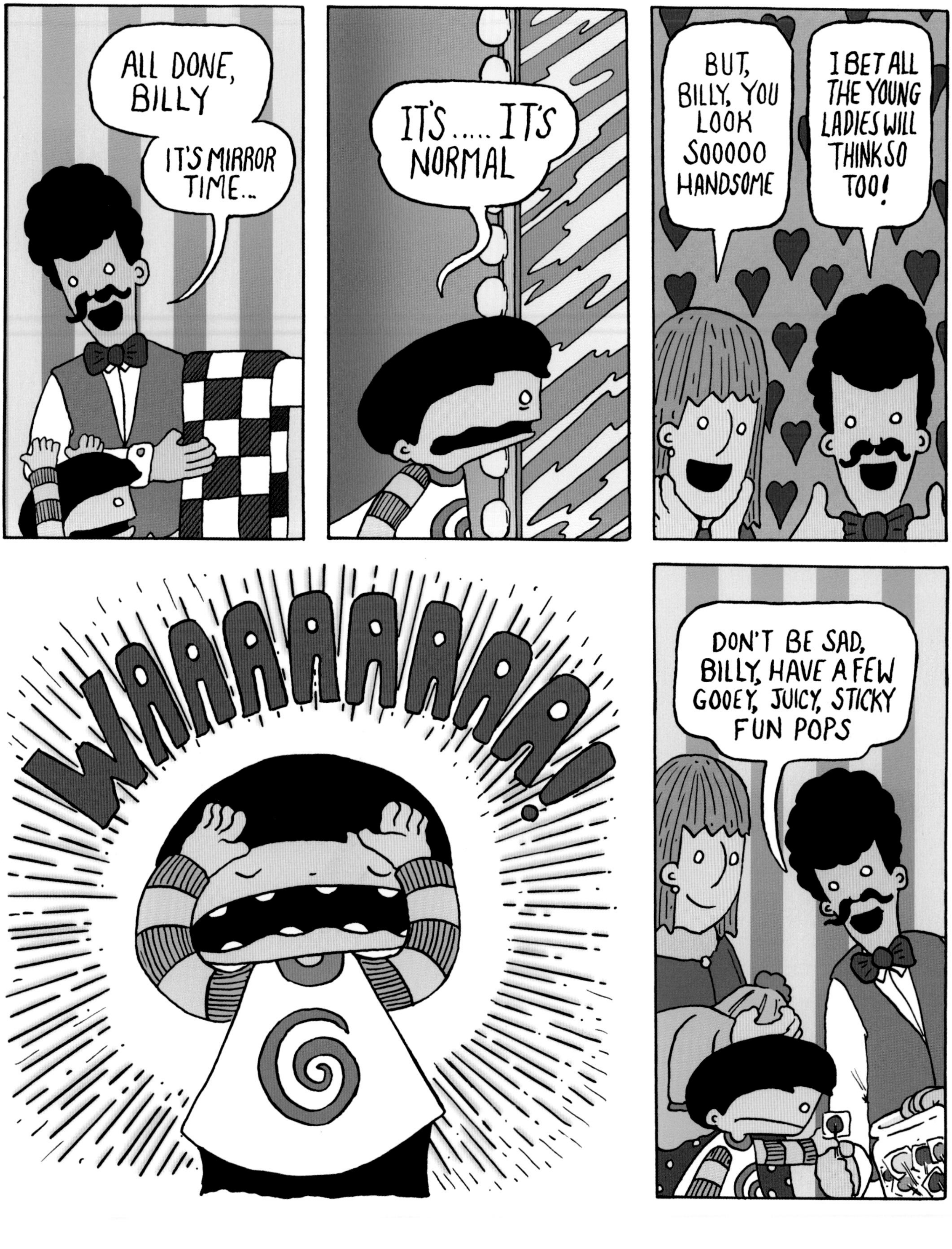
ALL DONE, BILLY
IT'S MIRROR TIME...
IT'S ..... IT'S NORMAL
BUT, BILLY, YOU LOOK SOOOOO HANDSOME
I BET ALL THE YOUNG LADIES WILL THINK SO TOO!
WAAAAAAAA!
DON'T BE SAD, BILLY, HAVE A FEW GOOEY, JUICY, STICKY FUN POPS

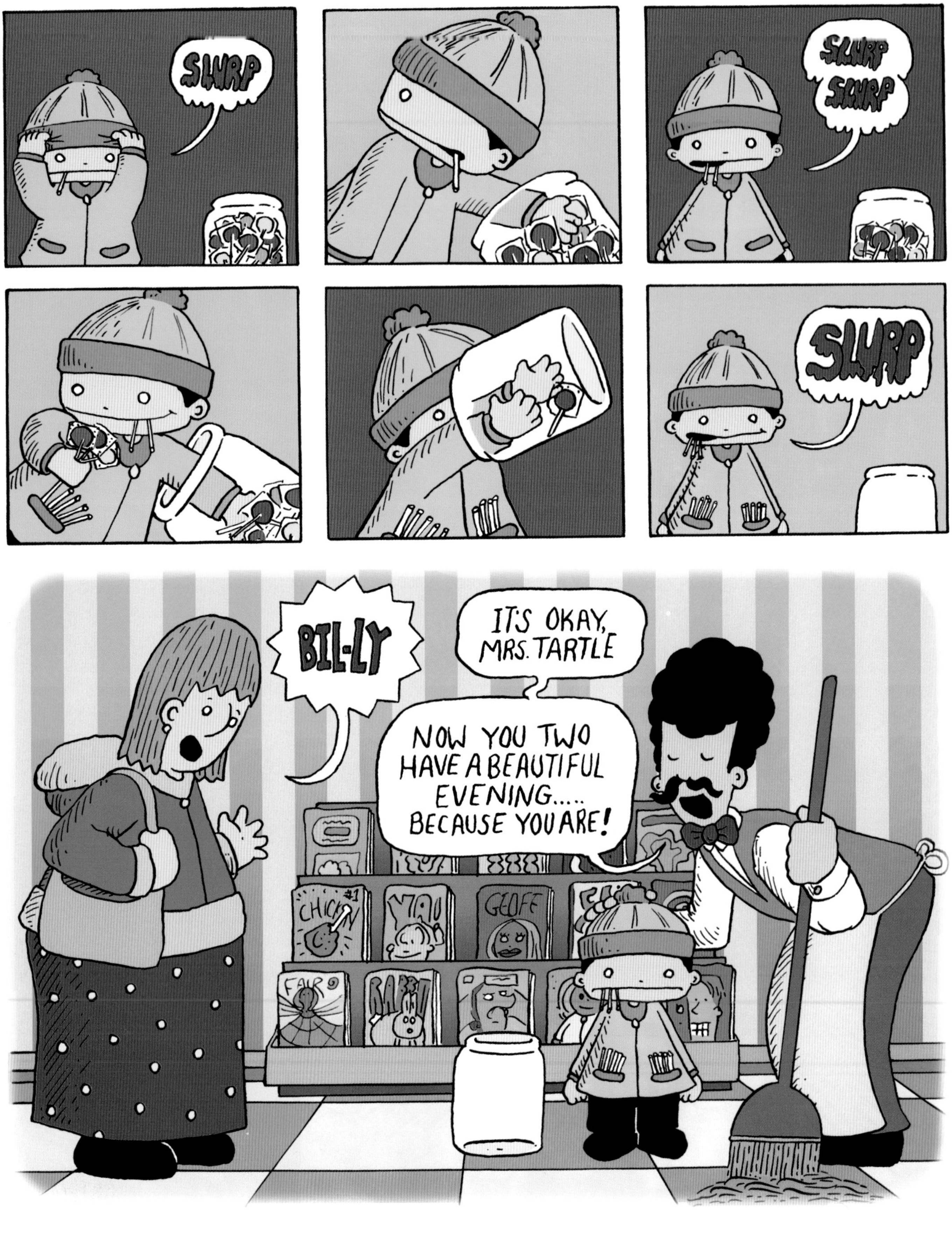
SLURP
SLURP
SLURP
SLURP
BIL-LY
IT'S OKAY, MRS. TARTLE
NOW YOU TWO HAVE A BEAUTIFUL EVENING..... BECAUSE YOU ARE!
CHICKEN #1
YAU
GEOFF
FAIR
RABBIT

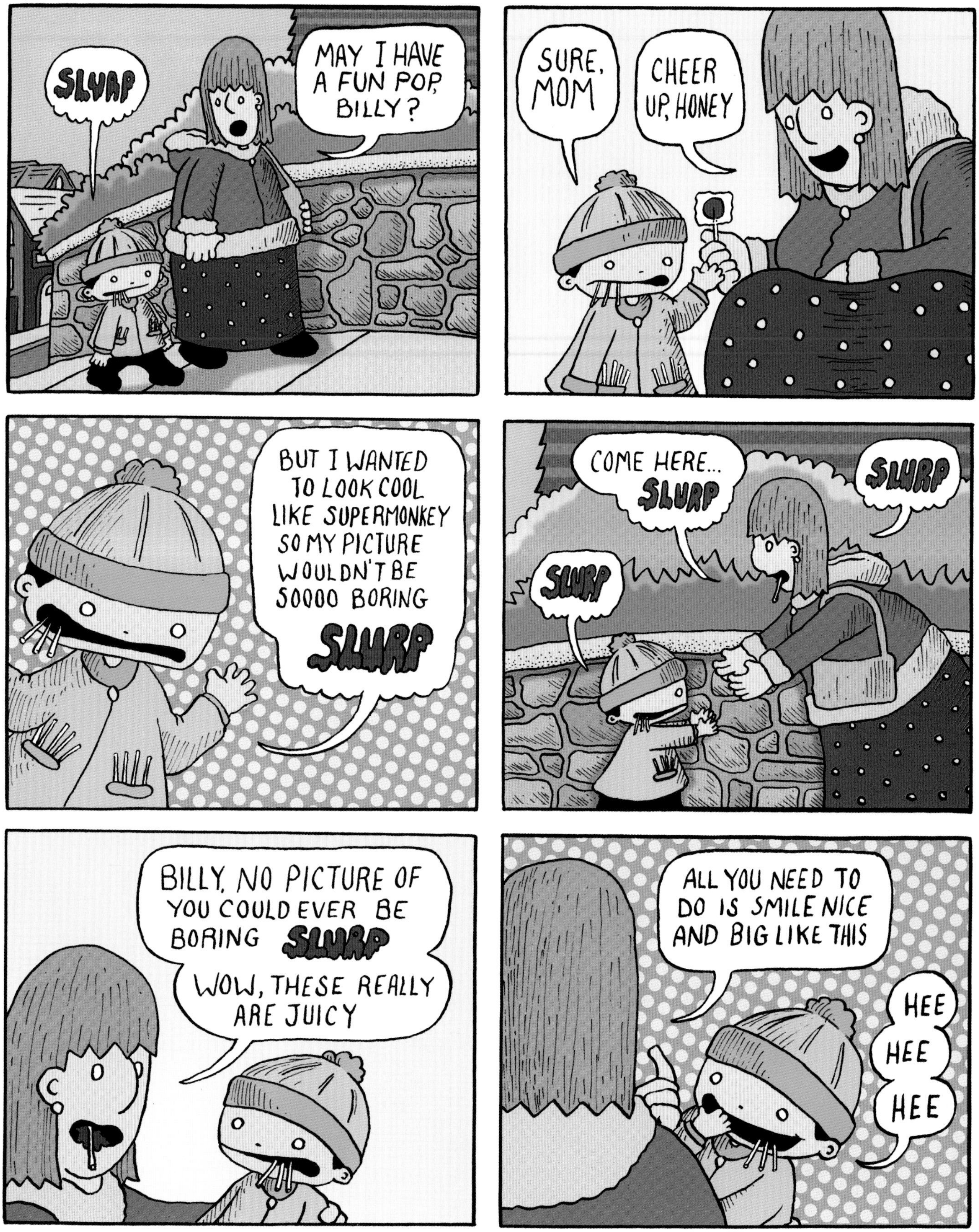
SLURP
MAY I HAVE A FUN POP, BILLY?
SURE, MOM
CHEER UP, HONEY
BUT I WANTED TO LOOK COOL LIKE SUPERMONKEY SO MY PICTURE WOULDN'T BE SOOOO BORING
SLURP
COME HERE... SLURP
SLURP
SLURP
BILLY, NO PICTURE OF YOU COULD EVER BE BORING SLURP
WOW, THESE REALLY ARE JUICY
ALL YOU NEED TO DO IS SMILE NICE AND BIG LIKE THIS
HEE
HEE
HEE

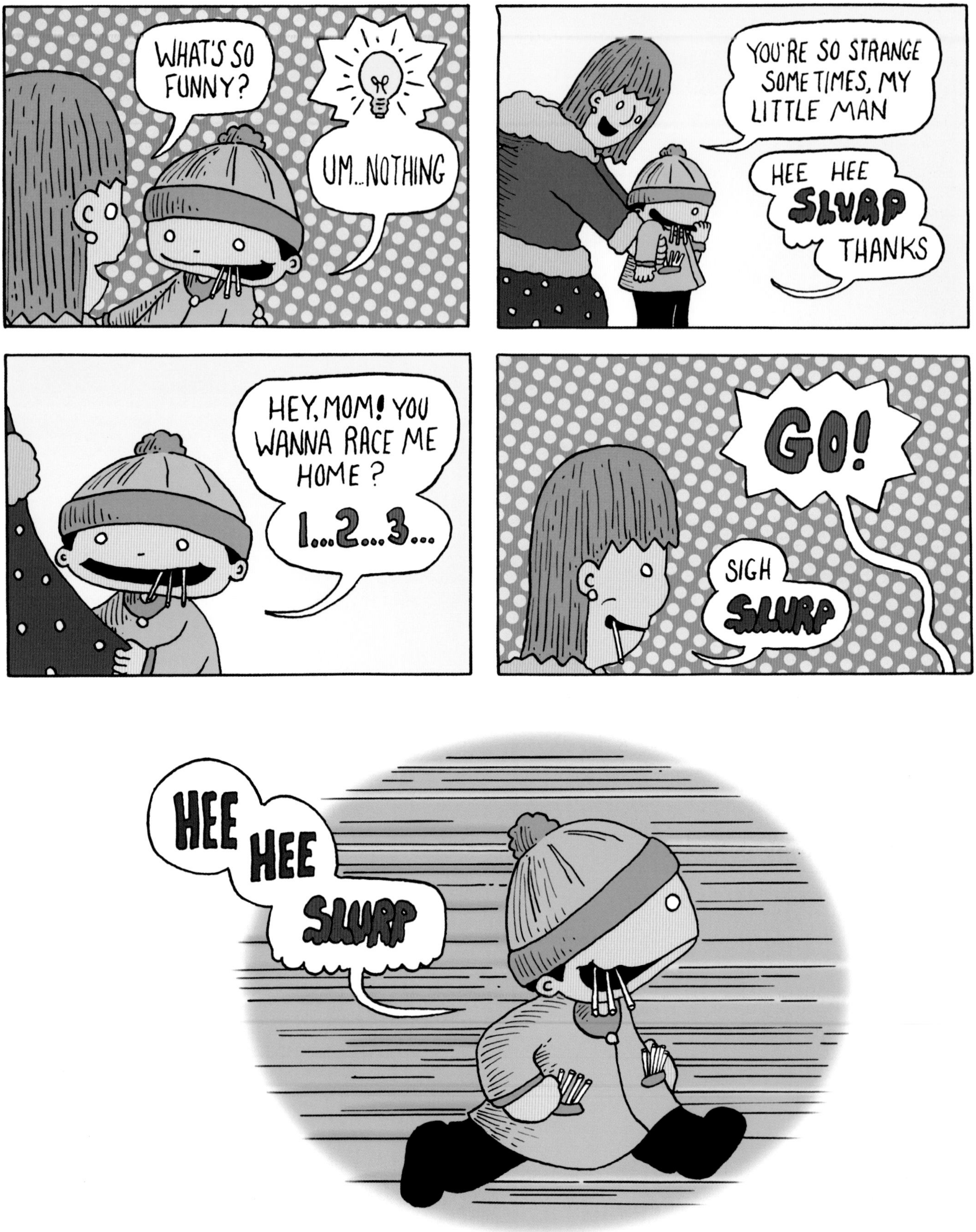
WHAT'S SO FUNNY?
UM...NOTHING
YOU'RE SO STRANGE SOMETIMES, MY LITTLE MAN
HEE HEE SLURP THANKS
HEY, MOM! YOU WANNA RACE ME HOME?
1...2...3...
GO!
SIGH SLURP
HEE HEE SLURP

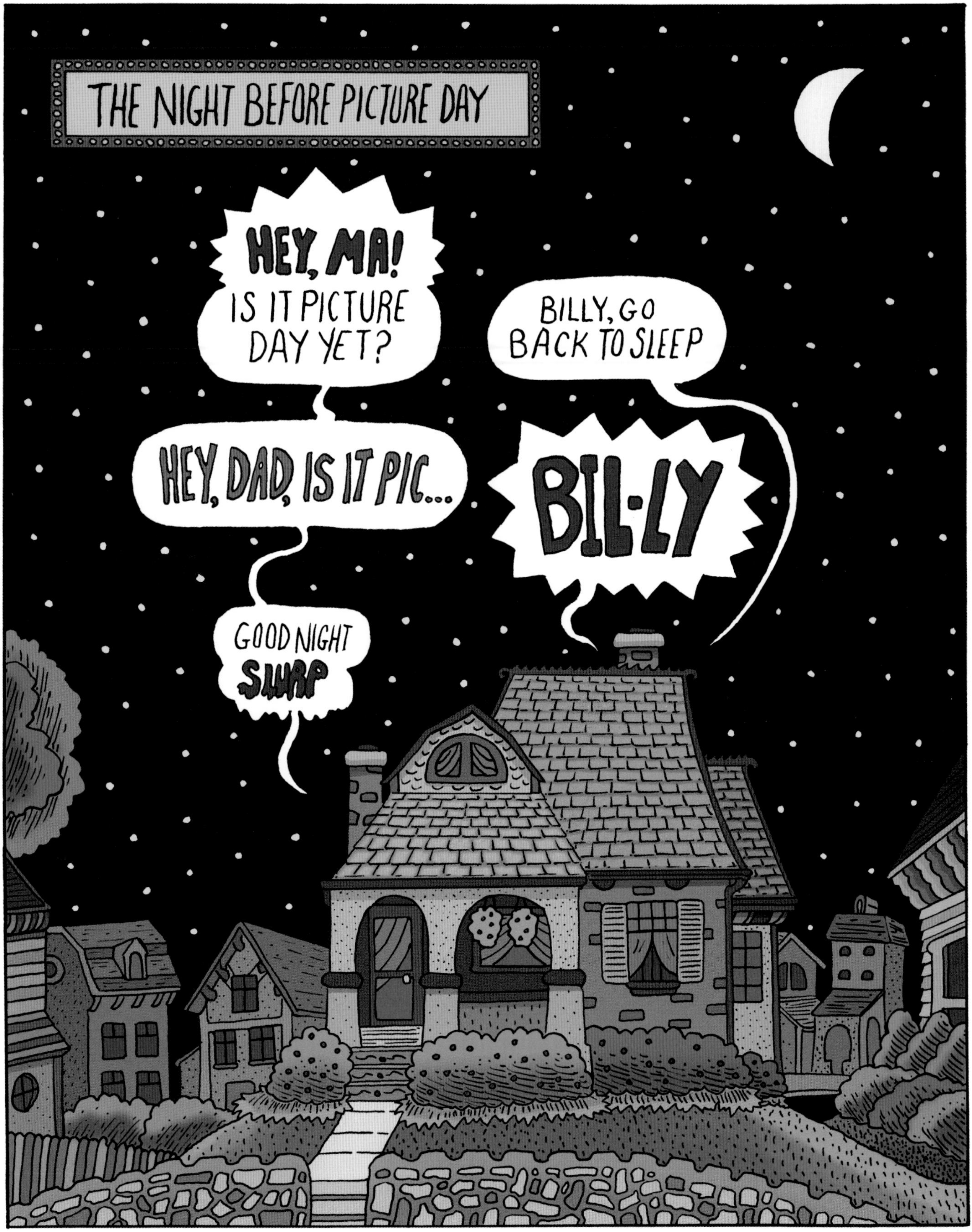
THE NIGHT BEFORE PICTURE DAY
HEY, MA! IS IT PICTURE DAY YET?
BILLY, GO BACK TO SLEEP
HEY, DAD, IS IT PIC...
BIL-LY
GOOD NIGHT SLURP

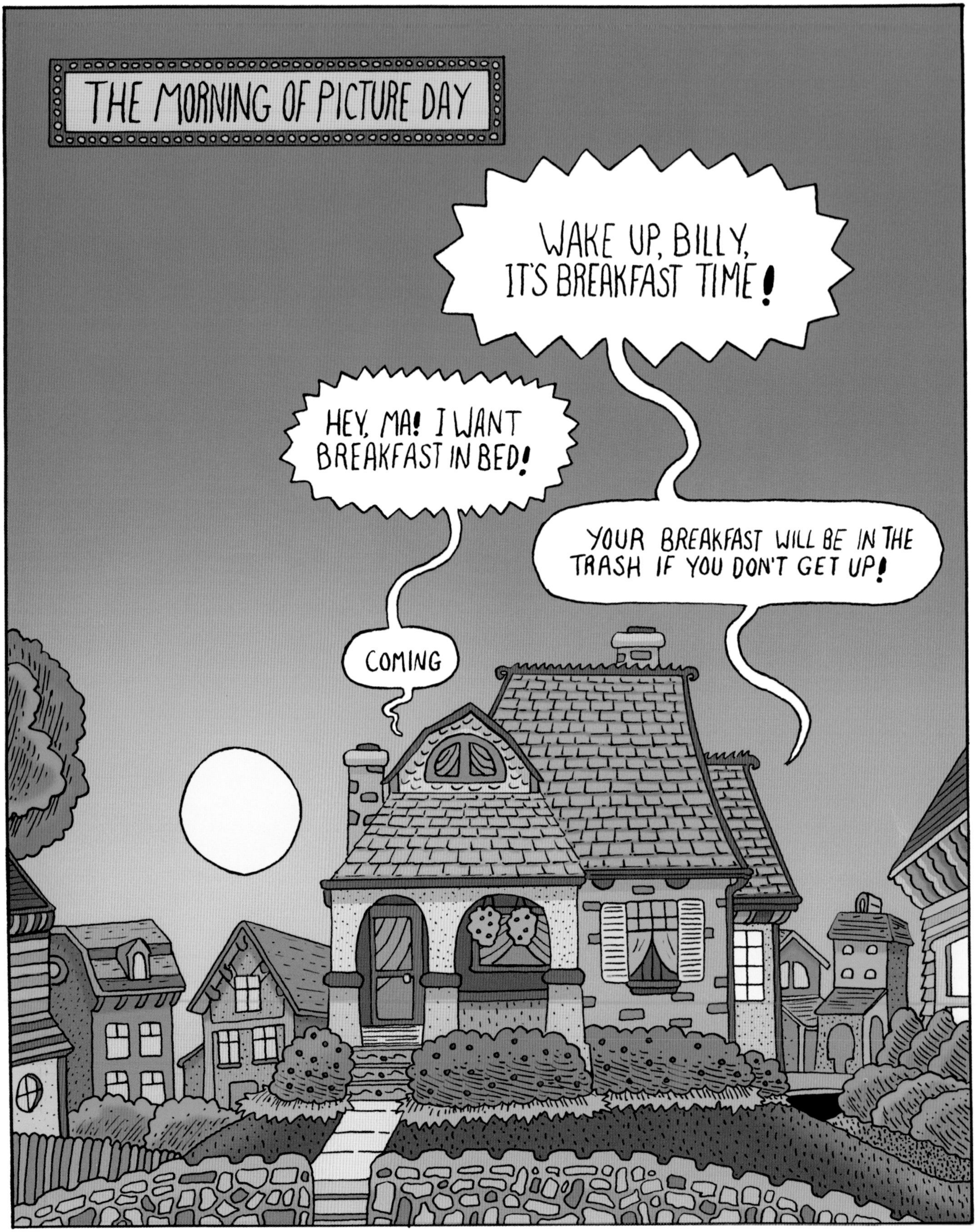
THE MORNING OF PICTURE DAY
WAKE UP, BILLY, IT'S BREAKFAST TIME!
HEY, MA! I WANT BREAKFAST IN BED!
YOUR BREAKFAST WILL BE IN THE TRASH IF YOU DON'T GET UP!
COMING

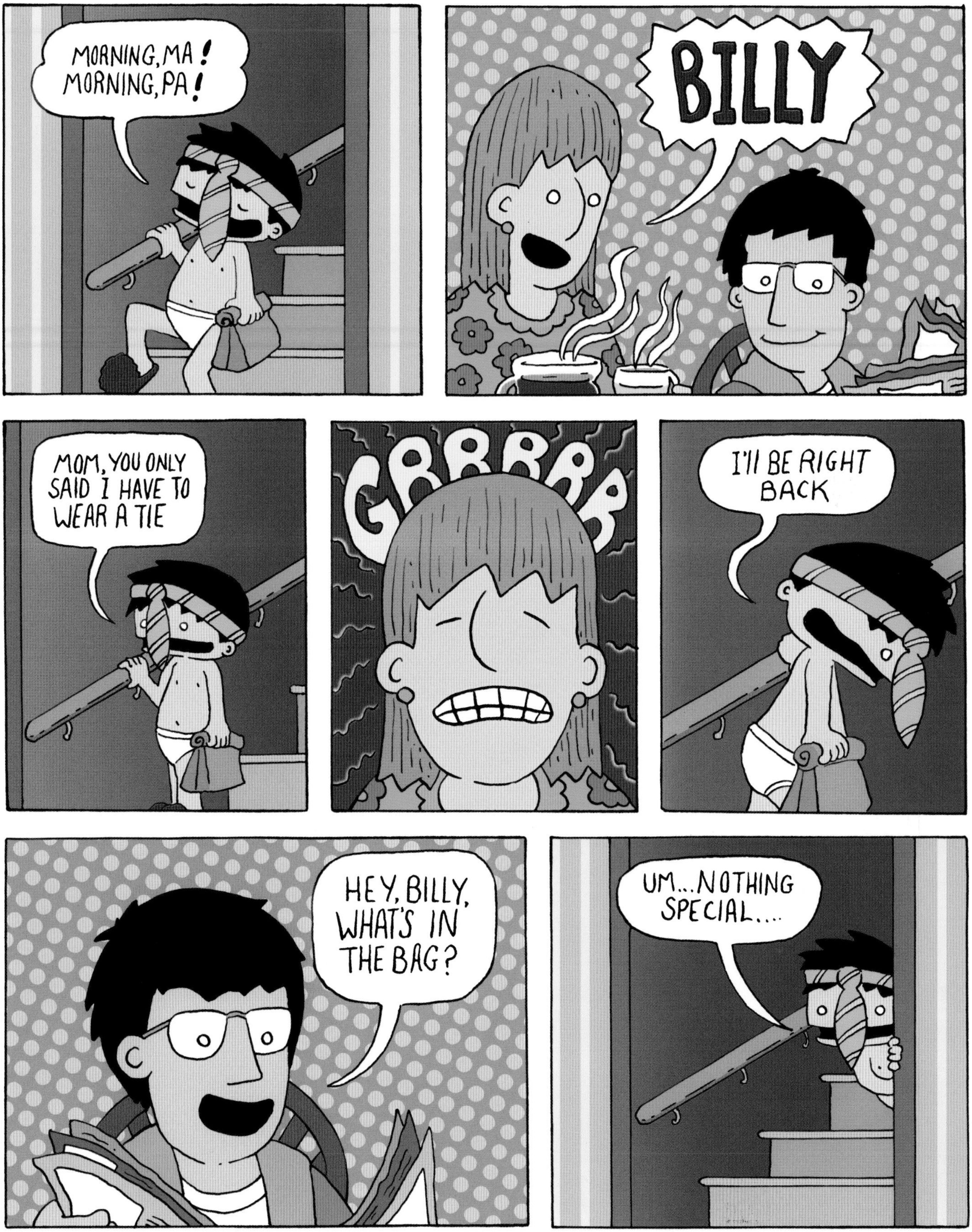
MORNING, MA! MORNING, PA!
BILLY
MOM, YOU ONLY SAID I HAVE TO WEAR A TIE
GRRRRR
I'LL BE RIGHT BACK
HEY, BILLY, WHAT'S IN THE BAG?
UM...NOTHING SPECIAL....

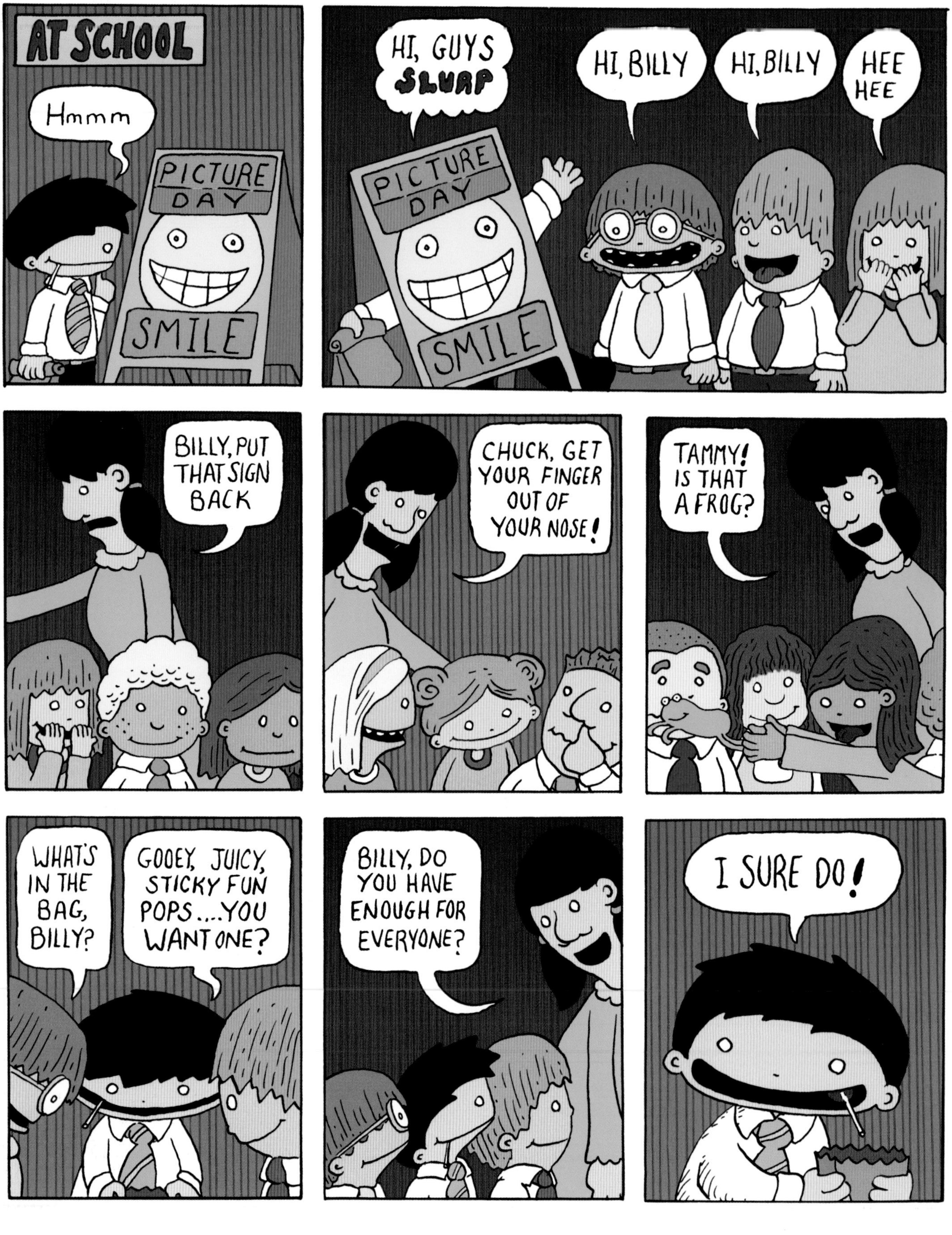
AT SCHOOL
Hmmm
PICTURE DAY
SMILE
HI, GUYS SLURP
HI, BILLY
HI, BILLY
HEE HEE
PICTURE DAY
SMILE
BILLY, PUT THAT SIGN BACK
CHUCK, GET YOUR FINGER OUT OF YOUR NOSE!
TAMMY! IS THAT A FROG?
WHAT'S IN THE BAG, BILLY?
GOOEY, JUICY, STICKY FUN POPS....YOU WANT ONE?
BILLY, DO YOU HAVE ENOUGH FOR EVERYONE?
I SURE DO!

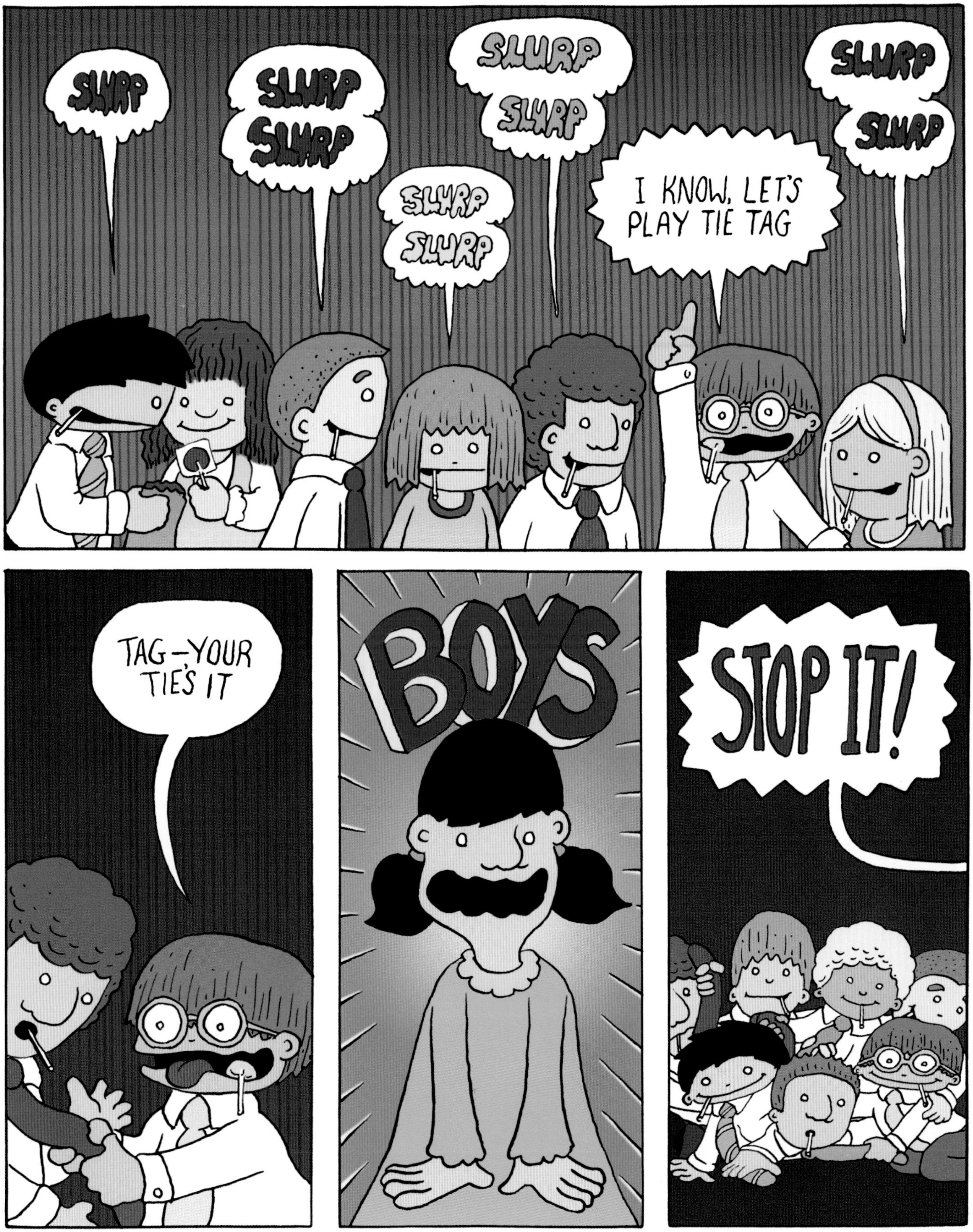
SLURP
SLURP SLURP
SLURP SLURP
SLURP SLURP
I KNOW, LET'S PLAY TIE TAG
SLURP SLURP
TAG—YOUR TIE'S IT
BOYS
STOP IT!

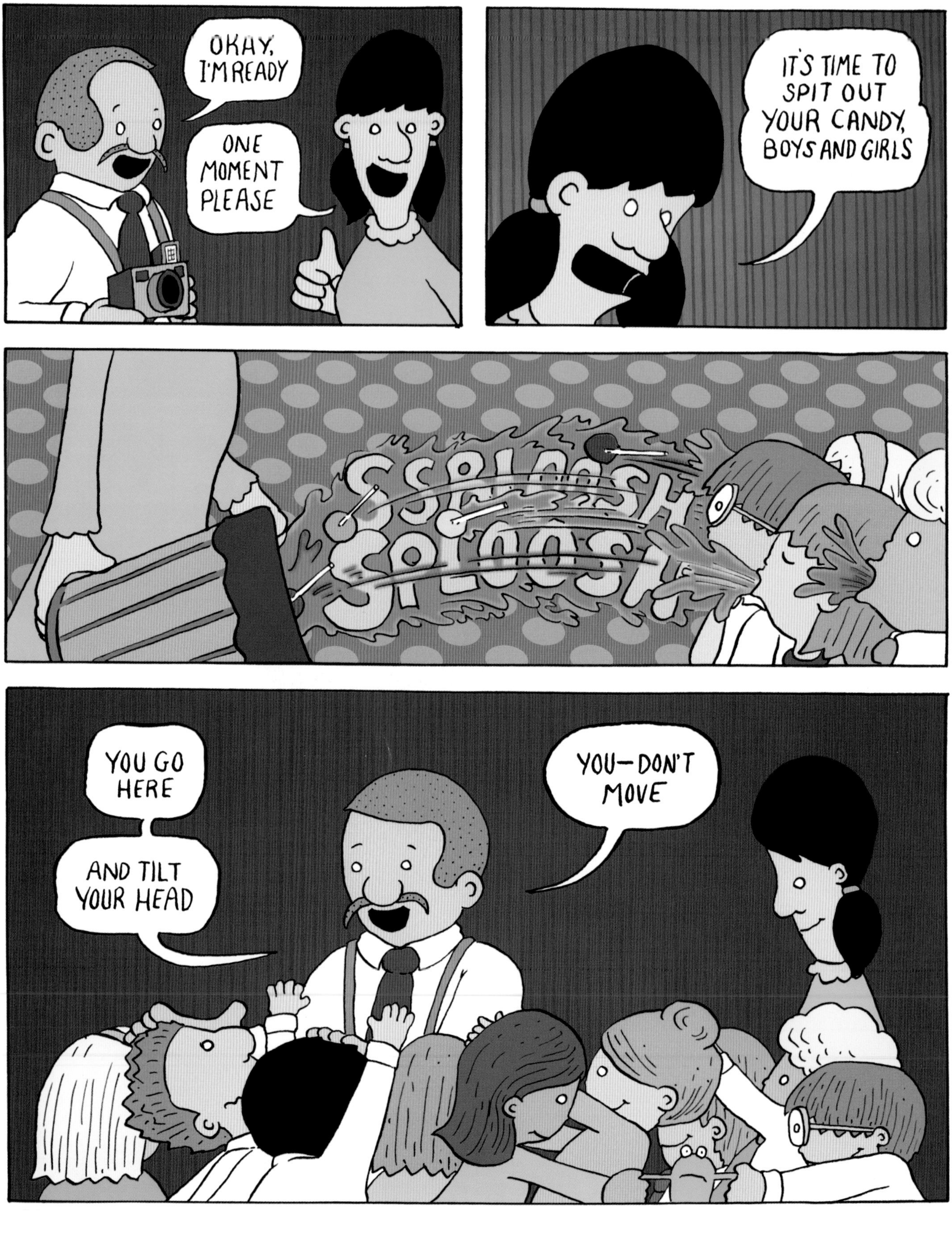
OKAY, I'M READY
ONE MOMENT PLEASE
IT'S TIME TO SPIT OUT YOUR CANDY, BOYS AND GIRLS
SSPLOOSH SPLOOSH
YOU GO HERE
AND TILT YOUR HEAD
YOU—DON'T MOVE

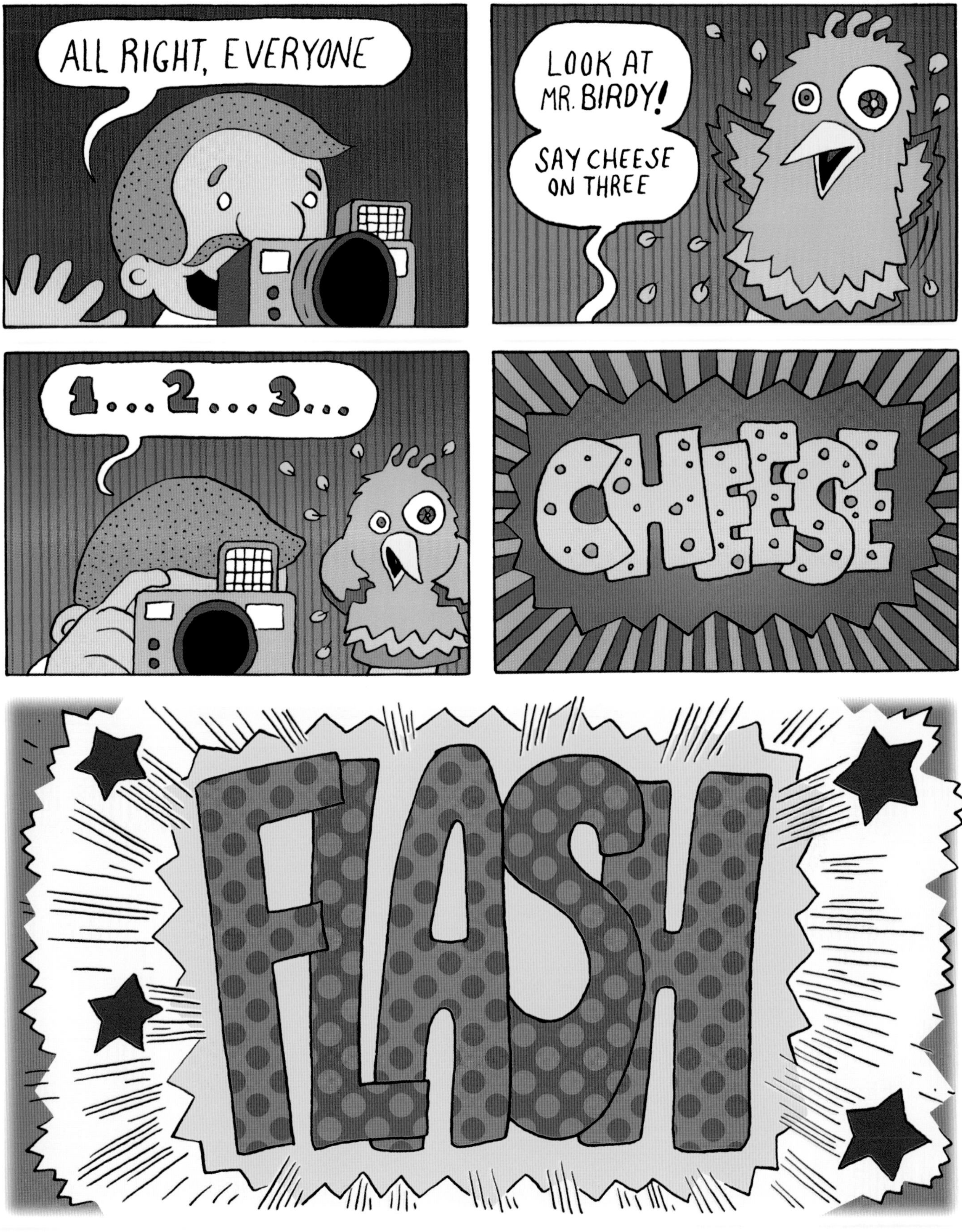
ALL RIGHT, EVERYONE
LOOK AT MR. BIRDY!
SAY CHEESE ON THREE
1...2...3...
CHEESE
FLASH

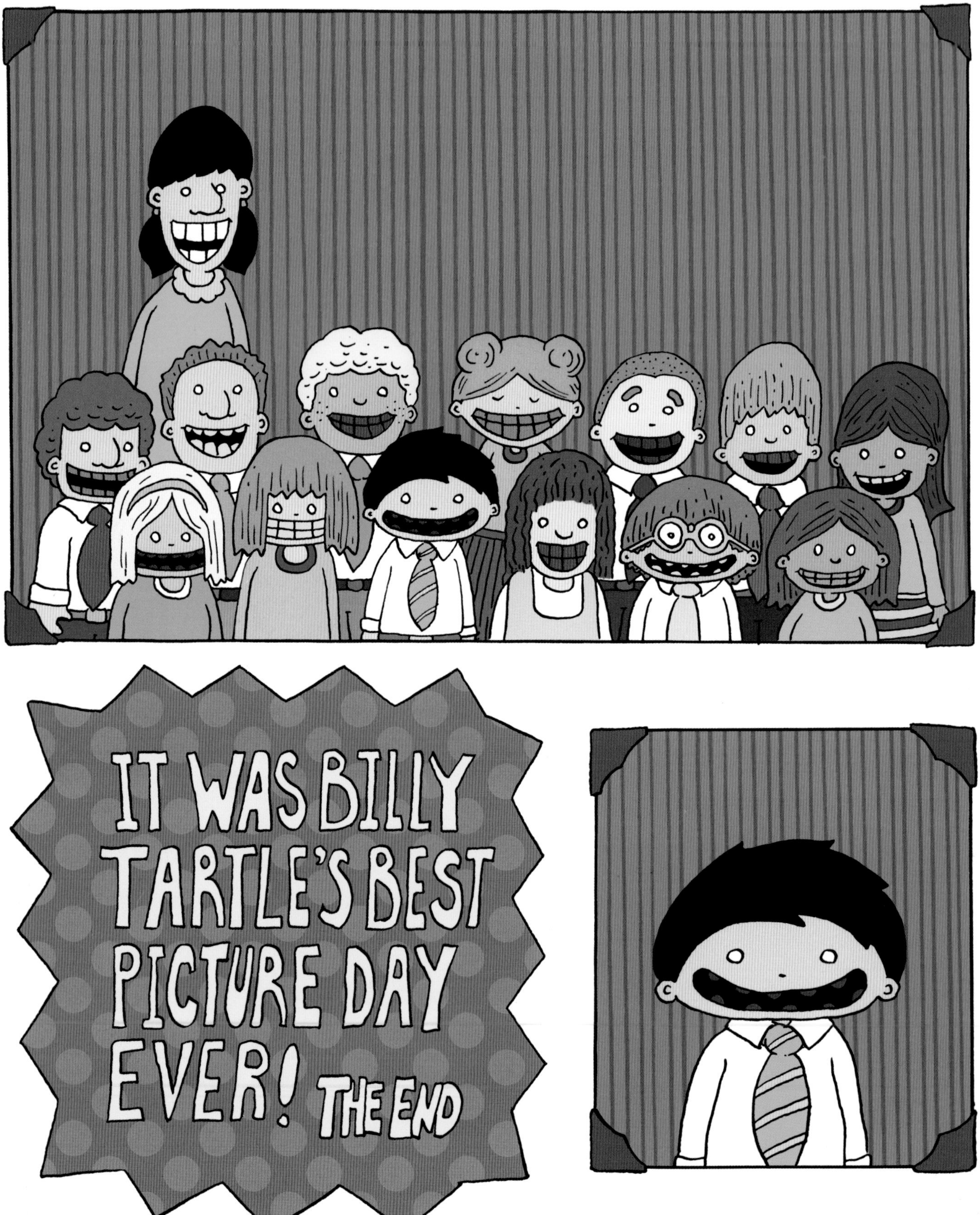
IT WAS BILLY TARTLE'S BEST PICTURE DAY EVER!
THE END

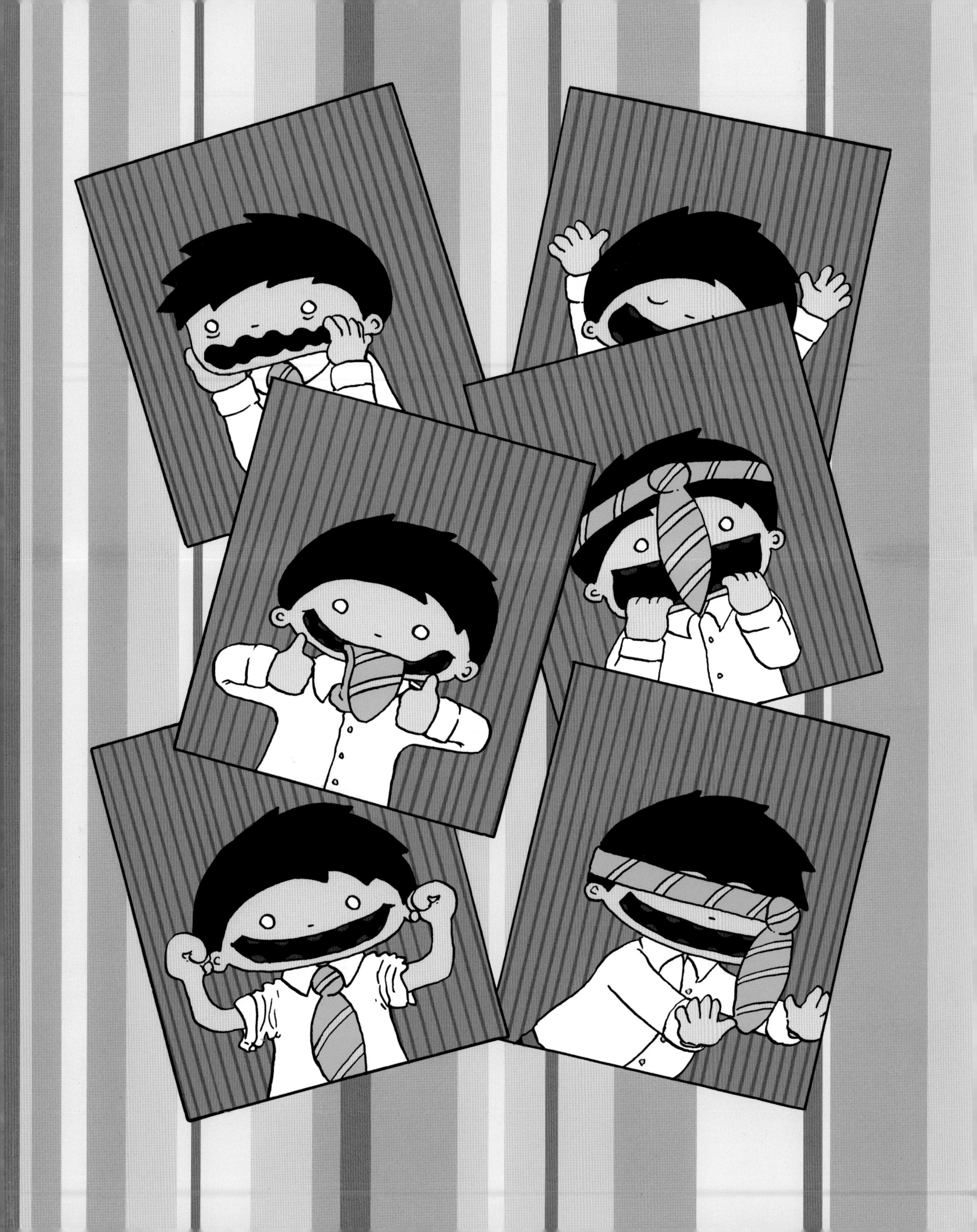

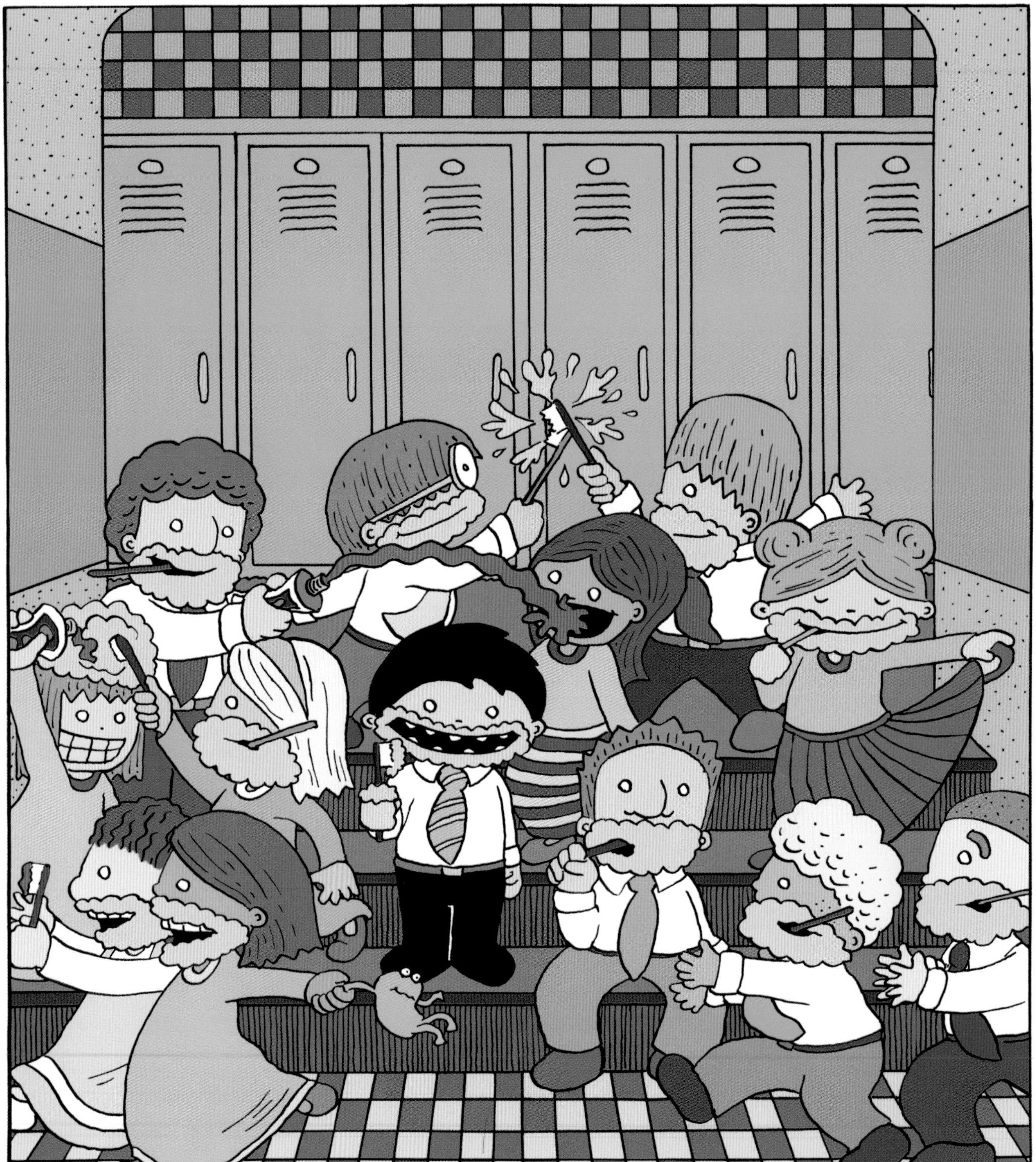